The Warrior Within

THE
WARRIOR
WITHIN

ANGUS McINTYRE

A TOM DOHERTY ASSOCIATES BOOK

NEW YORK

THE WARRIOR WITHIN

Copyright © 2018 by Angus McIntyre

Cover art by Martin Deschambault
Cover design by Christine Foltzer

Edited by Justin Landon

A Tor.com Book
Published by Tom Doherty Associates
175 Fifth Avenue
New York, NY 10010

www.tor.com

Tor® is a registered trademark of
Macmillan Publishing Group, LLC.

ISBN 978-0-7653-9709-6 (ebook)
ISBN 978-0-7653-9710-2 (trade paperback)

First Edition: March 2018

For Miranda

Acknowledgments

A book is never the work of just one person. My thanks go first of all to my editor, Justin Landon, who saw the potential in my story and then worked tirelessly to realize it. I also want to thank everyone else at Tor.com who helped him to transform the raw material into the polished final product that you have in your hands (or your ereader): publisher Irene Gallo, publicist Katherine Duckett, designer Christine Foltzer, and editor Carl Engle-Laird. Copy editor Bethany Reis disciplined my commas and restored coherence to a text written in a chaotic mix of British and American English. Artist Martin Deschambault took my vague descriptions and turned them into the stunning image you see on the cover.

Nadja Hicks, Sara Karnoscak, Joe Kennedy, Avi Kotzer, Wendy Mastandrea, Carlos Valcarcel, and Sally Woo all contributed essential feedback on early drafts of the novella. Marco Berta and Grazia Franzoni were kind enough to read a first draft of the climbing scene and point out all the obvious absurdities; the errors that remain are mine and mine alone.

My classmates from the 2013 Clarion Writer's Workshop—Jessica Cluess, Christian Coleman, Brandie Coonis, Thom Dunn, Sophia Echavarria, Zach Grafton, Brandon Haller, Kodiak Julian, Will Kaufman, Patrick Ropp, Gabriela Santiago, Matt Schnarr, Eliza Tiernan, Pieter van Tatenhove, Marie Vibbert, Alyssa Wong, and Isabel Yap—remain a constant source of inspiration, support, and encouragement. I am also forever indebted to our generous and brilliant instructors—Andy Duncan, Nalo Hopkinson, Robert Crais, Cory Doctorow, Karen Joy Fowler, Kelly Link, and Shelley Streeby—and to the Clarion Foundation.

I owe a lifetime debt of thanks to my parents, Colin and Field, and to my sisters, Mithra, Wayne, and Miranda, for all the love and support they have given me. Other friends and family members who have helped or inspired me over the years will need to wait for a longer book to receive the thanks that are their due. You know who you are.

Last and most of all, my thanks go to Melissa Ditmore, who encouraged me to write and gave me the space and time that I needed to do so. This book would not exist without her patience and generosity.

The Warrior Within

CHAPTER ONE

On the day after the Passing Festival, three men walked out of the swamps and came into town to kill a woman.

───────────

Normally, Karsman would have been one of the first to know about the strangers. But while the strangers were making their way across the salt flats that lay between the city and the distant marshes, Karsman was a good four or five kilometers away, heading out of town along the Road.

He walked hand in hand with a young woman. She had lilac hair, and fine gold wires were woven into the flesh of her right ear. The gray wind jacket that she wore was crisscrossed with colored ribbons. Her name was Mera, and he had known her for just two days and nights.

On the Road ahead of them, the vast wheeled bulk of a Temple advanced at slightly less than walking pace, towed by a dozen tractors, its spires and minarets stark against the hazy orange of the sky. Long strings of prayer flags flapped in the wind. Behind the Temple, a column of trucks and vans crept along in bottom gear, towing flatbed trailers laden with struts and panels: pieces of prefabricated housing that would be reassembled to make a new town somewhere farther down the Road. Young children stared sleepily from the cabs of the trucks and last night's revelers lay sprawled on top of the cargo like wounded soldiers being carried off the battlefield.

Karsman and Mera walked at the tail end of the procession, holding themselves a little apart from the other walkers.

"I should go back soon," said Karsman for the second or third time. Mera tightened her grip a little, holding on to his large hand possessively.

"Why?" she said. "Why not come with us?"

He considered the question. In truth, there was little enough reason to go back. The strip-town behind him was like any of a thousand others: not much more than a cluster of shacks thrown up along the fringes of the Road, huddled in the shadow of an abandoned Builder city. The only man-made structure of any solidity or size was the Temple, twin to the one now moving ponderously down the Road ahead of them. Even after twelve years, Karsman had few real attachments there—a handful of friends, some drinking companions, a couple of occasional lovers—no one he would really miss. The possessions he had left behind in his own shack would scarcely fill a small knapsack. Nothing he owned was worth the trouble of going back.

At the side of the Road, two young girls stood holding hands. They paid no attention to the crowd, which parted to move around them and closed up again. One of the girls had pushed her goggles up onto her forehead so that she could stare into her companion's eyes, and Karsman recognized her as the daughter of one of his neighbors. There was something so theatrically tragic about her expression that Karsman could not help smiling.

As he watched, she dropped the other girl's hand and turned away. Her lover stared after her for a few moments more, then shrugged, turned on her heel, and broke into a slow jog, hurrying to catch up to the trucks ahead.

It was the same at every Passing Festival. Temporary alliances formed during two days of revelry, then quickly dissolved as the passing Temple moved on down the Road. A few festival pairings became something more permanent. One person might choose to stay behind with a lover when the Temple left. Another would say good-bye to home and family and follow a new partner down the Road to an unknown destination, attaching themselves to a different Temple and making a new life in a new community. The arrangement might or might not last. Often, defectors simply drifted back after a few months, riding a road train back down the Road and picking up their lives again where they had left off.

Karsman had seen it all before. On a couple of occasions, he had considered the idea of moving on himself. But this was the farthest he had ever taken it, the farthest he had ever been from town since his arrival. He had the feeling that he was approaching a point of no return.

Mera tugged at his hand. "Come on," she said.

He let her lead him off the Road and up the slope of the windbreak. For most of its length, the Road ran level, raised no more than a half meter above the surrounding terrain. Here and there, however, great berms of concrete and earth were raised up on the sunward side of the roadway. Their inner faces were studded with niches that served as storm shelters. At their highest point, the windbreaks rose as much as eighty meters above the road, more than tall enough to protect even the tallest spires of a Temple from a gale blowing darkward.

Karsman and Mera sat down on the lip of the windbreak, feet dangling, watching the convoy roll slowly past below them. There were already a handful of other couples there, taking advantage of a last few moments together or simply admiring the view.

The view, such as it was, was made up of alternating stripes of color. Immediately below them lay the broad band of the world-girdling Road, its smooth black surface strangely resistant to the blowing dust that colored everything else a dull red. The Road ran arrow-straight all the way to the horizon in either direction, so flawless in its undeviating regularity as to seem almost unreal. Seen from above, it looked like a fissure splitting the planet in two.

On either side of the Road lay a wide strip of desert, dry red earth and rock, speckled here and there with grayish clots of dead vegetation. From the top of the windbreak it was possible to make out the irregular scratches of dry watercourses, like abstract writing on the arid ground. Rainstorms strong enough to fill them were rare. Over the years, the stream beds gradually filled with red dust and the wind blurred their outlines, softening and smoothing them until they blended back into the desert.

Far to sunward it was just possible to make out the beginning of the next band of color, a swathe of yellow-gray mudflats that marked the limits of the desert. From their present vantage point nothing else was visible, but Karsman had climbed some of the taller towers in the Builder city and knew that the banding continued. Beyond the mudflats lay a belt of swampland, visible as a confused scribble of contrasting textures: the black of floating vegetation mixed with glimmering patches of open water and the rusty knobs of outcrops. On rare clear days, you could sometimes see beyond the swamps to a white line of breaking waves and the red glint of the open ocean beneath a liquid shimmer of heat haze. Over it all hung the fat orange blob of the sun, perpetually hovering a few degrees above the horizon.

"So, why not come with me?" Mera asked.

Karsman shrugged. "I have—" He hesitated. "Responsibilities." He was aware of the absurdity of the phrase even before he finished speaking. He bit his lip, embarrassed by his own pomposity.

Mera, however, took him seriously. "Because you're the mayor," she said.

"I—what? No, that's just something they call me. It's more a joke than anything else."

Karsman's mayorship was entirely unofficial, his qualifications no more than a steady temperament and the willingness to occasionally thump a few heads together in the interests of keeping the peace. The local Muljaddy held the monopoly on spiritual and political power; the Temple guards were the only sanctioned wielders of coercive force.

"And you're not curious to see what's down the Road?" Mera continued.

He shrugged again. Privately, he doubted that whatever lay farther down the Road was any different to what he had already seen. He had traveled more than most, and all he had ever seen was the same red desert and dry scrub, the featureless black ribbon of the Road broken at intervals by windbreaks or the clusters of gaunt gray towers left by the Builders. And in the lee of the towers, the haphazard jumbles of strip-towns, each one much like another, anchored in place for a few years by a Temple and then packed up and trucked farther down the Road when the Temple's Muljaddy decided it was time to move on. Karsman had lived in a few strip-towns before he came to rest here. As far as he was concerned, there was little enough to choose between them.

He refrained from saying any of this, because once he started listing the ways that every place on the Road resembled every other place, he would eventually have to acknowledge that the only difference between this strip-town and the next would be the presence of Mera. Then he would have to tell her that that was not quite enough to convince him to pick up and move, and he had no wish to hurt her feelings. He genuinely liked her. She was smart and funny and spontaneous, and the last two days had been good. In the end, though, she was not quite enough to overcome his own inertia. Almost, but not quite.

He turned his head and looked back along the Road toward the towers of the Builder city, gray phantom shapes in the haze. Squinting, he could just make out a few tiny figures crawling on some of the higher galleries: scavengers, trying to pry loose a few crumbs of salvageable material or hoping to stumble on a hidden doorway to some section that hadn't already been picked over thirty times before. Tomorrow morning, he would be one of those ant-like figures. If he chose to go with Mera, then he would find himself on a different tower in a different city, but the work would be the same, the hard gray metal of the Builder towers no less unyielding.

The sight of the towers made up his mind for him. He stood up, brushing the dust from the seat of his coveralls.

"I should be getting back," he said.

Mera's face was unreadable, her eyes hidden by the scratched yellow plastic of her wind goggles.

"If you change your mind, you know where to look for me."

He nodded. "And if you change yours, I'll be here."

He stooped and kissed her lightly on the forehead. She squeezed his hand.

"Good luck, Karsman."

"Luck, Mera."

He turned and started to descend the slope of the berm, heading back toward the city. When he reached the Road, he glanced back. There was a figure standing on top of the windbreak, silhouetted against the sky, but he could not be sure that it was her.

When Steck finally found him, Karsman was sitting behind a windbreak at Kido's shop, picking through a handful of roasted sandnuts, trying to decide whether it was worth walking down to the Temple and turning a prayer wheel a few times to earn himself a better breakfast. He was dimly aware that something was happening outside, but in his present mood he felt no curiosity about it at all.

He cracked another nut between his teeth, spat fragments of shell into his hand, and popped the round gray core into his mouth. He sucked on it slowly, running his tongue over the fibrous surface.

"There you are," Steck said, putting his head around the corner of the windbreak.

"Here I am," Karsman agreed. He rubbed his hands together, scattering bits of broken shell on the ground.

"I thought you'd left town," Steck said, sounding slightly out of breath.

"I thought about it."

"Did you hear about the men?"

Karsman shook his head. "What men?"

"Coming out of the swamps." Steck pointed vaguely to sunward. "Three of them, walking together."

Karsman held the nut between his teeth for a moment, turning it around with his tongue.

"No one lives in the swamps," he said.

"Maroons do."

"Not round here," said Karsman. "And not for long anyway."

There were always a few people who rejected a life of dependence on one Temple or another and tried to strike out on their own, but maroon colonies seldom lasted more than a few months. Without a Temple to provide food and drinkable water, life was desperately harsh. Few food crops would grow in the dead, dry soil. The native plants—the fan weeds and watervines that covered the brackish waters of the swamps, the gnarled bushes of the brightside deserts—were all inedible, good for nothing more than raw mass in the Temple's converters. A few maroon colonies turned to banditry, preying on trucks along the Road until a Muljaddy sent Temple soldiers to hunt them down and crucify them as a warning to others. In the end, all the colonies failed, and any survivors crept back to the Road to be reintegrated into the closest strip-town.

"Maybe they're out-of-towners who overslept and forgot to leave with the rest," Karsman suggested.

Steck shook his head. "They're coming across the desert."

He sat down in the chair opposite Karsman. "You know how I've been working on that high spire, up on Tower Twenty-Four? There's this one finial there, right on the edge. If I can just expose the base plate, then I think I can get the whole thing free." He patted the cutting torch at his hip. "Anyway, I was up there this morning and I happened to look to sunward."

"And?"

"Well, I saw something moving. At first I thought it was just bits of dry weed picked up by the wind. But when I looked again, it was closer. And that's when I realized that they were actually moving toward the town."

"Men," said Karsman.

"Men, women, whatever. But human. Headed this way."

"Huh." Karsman cracked another nut.

"They came from the swamps," repeated Steck. "You should come and see."

"Why me?" asked Karsman rhetorically.

"You're the mayor," Steck said.

Karsman grunted. He tilted his head back and spat the husk of the nut over the windbreak.

"Very well," he said. "Take me there."

A small crowd had gathered at the edge of the Road, drawn up in a cautious semicircle about the three strangers. Karsman counted fewer than twenty people in all: most of the population of the strip-town were still in their shelters, sleeping off the excesses of the Festival.

The strangers appeared to be human, or at least close

enough to the human baseline to be counted as such. The one that Karsman took to be the leader was androgynously handsome, with strong, sculpted features and dark hair pulled back in a short ponytail. There was something almost foppish about his manner, but Karsman knew better than to let himself be deceived by appearances.

The second man was small and slightly built, with a narrow, forgettable face. But for the unusual cut of his clothes, he could have passed for a local, his skin and hair only a shade lighter than theirs. He held himself a little apart from the others, as if hoping to escape attention. Ignore me, his manner seemed to say. I'm not important.

The third man was not someone you could overlook. He was a pallid giant, taller even than Karsman and still broader across the shoulders. His shaven scalp was covered with a dense mass of tattoos. Like the others, he carried no weapons openly, but his long coat could have concealed a small arsenal. Instead of a dust mask, he wore a khaki scarf wrapped around the lower part of his face, and his eyes were invisible behind a narrow visor of smoked glass.

More than anything else, their clothing proved that they were not maroons. Instead of rags, they were dressed in close-fitting outfits with breeches and outer jackets of military cut. All three wore light packs and webbing harnesses hung with pouches and small pieces of equipment that Karsman could not immediately identify. Even unarmed, there was something unmistakably alert and martial about the way they stood. Karsman knew soldiers when he saw them.

Any conversation that had been going on before Karsman and Steck arrived had died away. A few of the men in the crowd held tools as if ready to use them as weapons, obviously distrustful of the strangers. They relaxed slightly as Karsman approached, relieved that the matter was now out of their hands.

The ponytailed leader registered the movement. He turned toward Karsman. "You, big man—are you in charge here?"

"Not me," said Karsman quickly.

The stranger continued as if he had not spoken. "Where can we get some food and a place to stay?"

"If you've got scrip to spend, at any of the shops along the Road," Karsman told him.

"And if we haven't?" asked the smaller of his two companions.

"You can go turn a wheel at the Temple."

The soldier's eyes narrowed, as if he suspected that he was being mocked.

"Is this your town?" he asked.

Karsman shook his head.

"So if you don't run the place, who does?"

"The Muljaddy, of course," Karsman said.

"What's a Muljaddy?" the stranger asked.

Someone in the crowd at his back tittered, then fell quickly silent as the soldier glanced their way.

One of Karsman's personas, the one he thought of as Diplomat, tried to come to the fore, but Karsman quickly pushed the persona back. He felt a momentary disorientation before Diplomat reluctantly unloaded itself and let Karsman take control of his own mind again. Diplomat would be the right choice, of course. Diplomat was all about nuanced communication, about smoothing out the rough spots and the misunderstandings. But Karsman had no desire to take on the role of emissary. Whatever was happening, he suspected it was better not to get involved. The star people could find their way to the Temple, and the Muljaddy could deal with them. It was none of his business.

"You're not from here, are you?" said Steck. "Are you off a starship?"

The stranger turned to look at him. "That's right."

There was a ripple of movement in the crowd, as if the onlookers were uncertain whether to draw closer to the visitors or to pull back to a safer distance. "So why are you here?" asked one of the bolder spirits.

"We're here," the stranger said, "to kill a woman."

———

"They're soldiers, aren't they?" said Steck as he and Karsman walked back toward Kido's.

"Of a kind." Karsman glanced back over his shoulder to verify that the three strangers were still walking the other way, headed down the road toward the Temple. A few curious townspeople followed them, keeping their distance.

"Could you take them?" asked Steck.

Karsman stopped. "What?"

"Could you beat them in a fight?"

Karsman shook his head in exasperation. "Steck, I don't think you understand what soldiers are. Me, I'm a brawler. Round here, I pass for a tough guy. But those three are professional killers. They're biohacked, chipped and wired. They can butcher you nine different ways while you're still thinking about where to land the first punch. I wouldn't last fifteen seconds."

Don't sell yourself short, said Warrior, his speech a flicker of aggression in Karsman's head. You and me, like old times. We could take the big one out, no problem. You saw the way he stood. Size always makes them sloppy. They get used to winning fights by sheer muscle and mass. Overconfidence kills.

And what if he has a Warrior of his own? Karsman asked. He felt a tremor of hesitation from the persona.

We're better, Warrior insisted.

You don't know that, said Karsman. What were you

saying about overconfidence?

"Which one is the most dangerous?" asked Steck.

"Huh?"

"The soldiers. Which one do you think is the most dangerous?"

Karsman shunted Warrior to the back of his mind.

"I don't know," he said. "The little guy, maybe. Or the one with long hair."

Steck stopped and looked at him, frowning. "Not that huge guy?" he asked. "He's bigger than you are."

Karsman shrugged.

"Maybe," he conceded, unwilling to go into his reasons. "Listen, Steck, they're all dangerous. You stay away from them. Tell everyone else to do the same. Any idiot who gets in their way is going home dead."

"Do you think they're really off a starship?"

"Probably."

"And they came all this way just to kill a woman?"

"That's what they said."

"Why would they do that?" Steck asked.

Karsman did not answer. He had been wondering the same thing himself.

CHAPTER TWO

Karsman passed a restless night, tossing and turning on his pallet. When he woke the next morning, he was still tired, his muscles aching as if he had not rested at all. A vague sense of foreboding hung over him. That feeling of impending doom puzzled him until he remembered the three soldiers who had walked out of the desert the afternoon before. Trouble, he thought gloomily.

He lay on his bed, staring up at the pressed plastic ceiling of his shack. Perhaps the assassins had already done their work and moved on. Maybe their intended victim was at the Temple. He wondered if they had assassinated the Muljaddy. The Muljaddy was the only person in town that Karsman could imagine as being of sufficient importance to merit the attention of three hitmen from off-world.

Technically, this Muljaddy was neither male nor female, but maybe the soldiers' culture did not make the distinction. The more Karsman thought about it, the more he liked the idea. It was not that he felt any particular ill will toward the Muljaddy, or even toward the Muljaddy family in general. They were the rulers of the world, and nothing Karsman did or thought could change that. But it would make matters simpler if whatever business had brought the soldiers here involved the aristocracy rather than any of Karsman's friends or neighbors.

There had been a time in his life when Karsman had briefly entertained ideas of revolution. In his youth he had traveled off-planet, part of the entourage of a different Muljaddy. That brief exposure to a wider universe had opened his eyes in a number of ways. Among other things, he had been startled to learn that rule by a single family was not the inevitable order. He had been still more surprised to learn that the Muljaddy family that held such sway here were the smallest of small fish on a galactic scale. For a time, that discovery led him to all kinds of strange thoughts. Despite never having had the slightest political education, he quickly arrived at his own rudimentary model of democracy and began wondering how it might be applied at home.

The brief revolutionary fervor burned out almost as quickly as it came. He soon also learned that there were worse forms of tyranny than the rule of the Muljaddy, who demanded little more than formal obedience and at least token adherence to the religion they preached. It became clear to him that trying to replace a relatively benign dictatorship was a potentially perilous undertaking.

More to the point, he had recognized the futility of trying to preach revolution to people who had no conception that any other form of existence was possible. Aside from the maroons, no one chafed particularly under Muljaddy rule. They simply accepted it, in the same way that they accepted that the sun was always visible at more or less the same place in the sky, that the winds blew more or less constantly, and that the world was divided into zones of light and dark. It was the way things were. When Karsman returned home, he put aside the notions that he had acquired and took up the placid fatalism of his compatriots again. It was just easier that way.

So he had no particular desire to see the soldiers kill the Muljaddy or anyone else at the Temple. Still, he would have preferred any bloodshed to happen there rather than in the strip-town. His real fear was that he might be called upon to do something, something that might bring him into lethal conflict with the three killers. Karsman's unofficial mayorship might not have a salary attached, but it did come with an implicit obligation to act as a general peacemaker, arbitrator, and occasional policeman. If any trouble started with the soldiers, his neighbors would expect him to resolve it, and Karsman was not optimistic about the likely outcome. Whatever Warrior pretended, Karsman knew when he was outclassed.

So all in all, the idea that the whole affair might play out at a level far above him was very attractive. Let the soldiers try to kill the Muljaddy. Perhaps they would succeed, perhaps the guardians of the Temple would kill them first. Whatever the outcome, Karsman and the few people who he cared about would be sheltered from the storm. When the soldiers moved on, their job done, a new Muljaddy would arrive from the capital and life would go on as before. It was, Karsman thought, probably the best thing for everyone.

He got up stiffly and splashed some tepid water on his face. He felt relieved, and suddenly hungry.

His newfound good humor lasted only until he reached Kido's. When he pulled open the door of the shop, the first thing that he saw were three unfamiliar backs huddled in front of the tiny bar.

He stood there stupidly, his hand still on the door handle. A gust of wind fluttered the ribbons that dangled from the ceiling. He caught a glimpse of Kido behind the bar, a worried expression on his face. There were no other patrons inside.

Karsman pushed the door slowly closed and took a step back. He did not think that Kido had seen him. He could not be so sure about the soldiers. At least some of the three almost certainly had augments that would have told them of his presence. Perhaps they had scattered spy-eyes around the place. Sitting with their backs to the door might have been a deliberate gesture, intended to demonstrate that they feared no one here, but he doubted that they would really have been so unprofessional as to leave themselves truly unguarded.

Guys who do that don't last long, agreed Warrior.

He let Warrior off the leash for a moment, allowing his heightened awareness to scan around him for possible devices. Like the other personas, Warrior was a specialist. An expert in personal defense, he would pick up clues that Karsman himself would miss.

To Karsman's surprise, Warrior found no sign that the soldiers had prepared a perimeter.

Amateurs, Warrior said.

Or true professionals, Karsman said. Just because you don't see it doesn't mean it isn't there.

If I don't see it, it isn't, said Warrior.

Maybe.

He flipped Warrior back to background, leaving just enough of the persona's consciousness resident in his mind to alert him to danger and allow him to react rapidly. He never liked running any of his personas fully in parallel, least of all Warrior. Karsman running Warrior was aggressive and impulsive. If Karsman let Warrior have his way, he'd probably want to take the soldiers on here and now.

But at least running the personas in parallel rather than ceding control entirely left him some measure of control. That way he could rein in Warrior's worst impulses. What Karsman feared most was that some emergency would trigger one of his personas to take full control. He hated the feeling of being submerged in his own mind. He hated the sensation of losing control. He hated the doubts it raised: perhaps the identity that he thought of as "I" might be just another persona, maybe not even the original. But most of all, he hated returning to consciousness with no awareness of the passage of time and no memory of anything he had done while backgrounded. Whichever persona had taken control, it was always Karsman who had to deal with the consequences. And when the persona in question was Warrior, the consequences might include corpses.

He waited until he was a good distance from Kido's and then switched Warrior out entirely, reducing him to no more than a flicker of awareness at the back of his mind. As he did so, he remembered again that he was hungry. With Kido's closed to him, there was only one place where he could find breakfast. He stuck his hands in his pockets, hunched his shoulders against the wind, and started down the Road toward the Temple.

———————

The Temple was dark and warm, its corridors and spaces heavy with the smell of incense and oil. Despite his lack of religious convictions, Karsman always found it soothing. He stood on the threshold and let the warmth and the odors and the muffled sound of the chanting from the main hall wash over him.

He thought about going down and joining the ongoing service. Today was sacred to the goddess Arinna, Karsman's favorite of the nine gods. The sculptors always gave her statues a rather ambiguous expression that Karsman liked. He thought it made her look less aloof than her peers, perhaps even a little roguish. If she were a flesh-and-blood woman, she would be good company, he thought, the kind who might share a drink and then slip into bed with you for a good-natured, friendly fuck. His type of goddess, in short.

But joining the service would mean being around other people, and this morning he wanted to be alone. Instead of going down into the main hall, he climbed the stair that led to one of the side corridors on the upper level.

The corridor was almost completely dark. The only

light came from a line of tall prayer wheels set in niches along the wall, each drumlike wheel glowing with its own internal illumination.

He chose a wheel close to the far end of the corridor. A speaker beside it relayed the sound of chanting from the main hall at a level scarcely greater than a whisper. He pressed his hand to the touch plate on the wall beside the wheel and waited a moment for the system to acknowledge his presence, then knelt down and grasped the handle that turned the wheel. The metal was cool to the touch, worn smooth by countless hands over the decades.

Turning the wheel was a pleasant, repetitive activity that required no thought. In theory, the worshipper was supposed to repeat the words of the prayer printed on the wheel or recite a mantra, but Karsman preferred to let his mind go blank, losing himself in the simple, mechanical motion of turning the handle. In any case, the act was supposed to be effective whether one prayed or not, the words of the printed prayer flying from the slowly turning cylinder up to the ear of whichever god was depicted in bas-relief above the niche.

The chanting from the hall below died away. There was a moment of silence and then he heard the shuffle of the congregation kneeling, followed by the call-and-answer that announced the beginning of the sermon. Karsman started to pay more attention. He was curious to know what the Muljaddy might have to say about the newcomers.

The sermons never deviated much from the same general pattern. In the first part, the preacher would enumerate the sufferings of the worshippers in this imperfect world. The second consisted of general praise for the beneficence of the deity of the day. The third and final part was an appeal for intervention and the prompt transportation of the deserving faithful to the appropriate paradise.

Interwoven with all this were laudatory references to the Muljaddy of the Temple and the larger family to which they belonged. Doctrine said that every Muljaddy was personally sinless. It was only their compassion for the people that kept them all from ascending to the better world that was their personal due, and it was only the sins of the people that made this compassion and guidance necessary. The subtext of the sermons was always that the people needed to hurry up and better themselves so that the Muljaddy could be released from the burden of caring for them.

Karsman was not much interested in the sermons for themselves. What interested him was that they also functioned as a kind of news broadcast, more opaque than town gossip, but more informed on certain matters. They were a window into the mind of the Muljaddy and the Temple hierarchy, reflecting current concerns and containing subtle admonitions to their followers. Ever since he had ceased to pay attention to the religious message, Karsman had become increasingly adept at disentangling the other messages contained in each sermon. If there was something that the Muljaddy wanted everyone to know or think about the soldiers, it would be in the sermon.

But if he hoped for a revelation, Karsman was disappointed. The junior priest who delivered the sermon appeared to have nothing to say about the soldiers at all. He mumbled through the usual litany of sufferings, the requisite praise, and the appeal for intervention without deviation or digression. However Karsman looked at it, there was nothing in the sermon that he could interpret as an allusion to the presence of strangers in town. Did this lacuna reflect a wait-and-see policy, a cautious refusal to take any definite position on the outsiders until the situation became clearer? Or could the Muljaddy actually be unaware that something extraordinary was happening? He frowned, puzzled.

He looked down at the revolution counter at the base of the prayer wheel. He had completed enough turns to entitle him to a cup of broth, which would take the edge off his hunger. But if he continued to turn the wheel, the accumulated credit might be used to buy something more substantial. He hesitated, considering his options.

In the time it took him to make up his mind, his decision was made for him. The priest chanted the closing prayer, and Karsman heard the sound of the hall below emptying out. If he went down now, he would need to stand in line behind all the other worshippers queuing for the food that their devotions had earned them. He sighed, settled himself more comfortably on his kneeler, and started to turn the wheel again.

───────────

When Karsman looked in at Kido's later, the three strangers had gone. The little shop was empty of customers. Kido was sitting behind the bar with his chin in his hands.

"No food, Karsman," he said as Karsman entered.

"I'll have a drink then," Karsman told him, settling himself at the bar. It was really too early in the day to begin drinking, but the events of the last two days had left him feeling on edge. A drink would settle him down and get him in the mood to begin working again. Sometimes he needed the mild buzz of alcohol to take the edge off the tedium of toiling over broken machinery or trying to chisel off fragments of old Builder structures to sell as salvage to the Temple.

"No drinks either," Kido said. His broad face was glummer than Karsman had ever seen it.

Karsman eyed the full bottles behind the bar. Kido brewed his own booze using food scraps bought from the Temple. It was crude stuff, raw and potent.

"What are you talking about, Kido?"

"Those guys. They've forbidden me to sell anything. They said that I had to keep everything I had for them, and only them." Kido pointed an accusatory finger at Karsman. "You were the one who told us we should do what they said."

"I didn't say that you were to let them tell you to cut off your best customers," protested Karsman.

"So what are you going to do about it?"

Karsman said nothing. After a moment, Kido relented.

"Because it's you, Karsman," he said. "But no one else can hear about it." He took a bottle down from the shelf and pushed it across the bar toward Karsman.

Probable audio and video bugs, said Warrior.

Karsman stopped in the act of reaching for the bottle. He shook his head. "No, Kido," he said loudly. "It's best if you do as they say." He shrugged his coat back on. "Give them what they want. If we don't give them any trouble, they'll go on their way and everything will go back to normal. Got it?"

"Got it." Kido sounded puzzled as he set the bottle back on the shelf.

Coward, said Warrior.

CHAPTER THREE

The trouble Karsman had been anticipating came faster than he expected.

He was resting after a day spent in the packing yard, heaving salvaged tiles and piping onto pallets, ready to be loaded onto the next road train and trucked down the Road to the capital. It was punishing work, but he was glad to be able to lose himself in it, his mind empty while his body labored.

A rapid knocking roused him from a light doze. He rolled over, doing his best to ignore it. Finally, when the knocking showed no sign of stopping, he got up and went to open the door.

Little Alya, Dijah's youngest child, looked up at him. Her face was pinched with fear. "Those men," she said. "They're at my mam's place. I think they've killed Doro."

Karsman muttered a curse under his breath.

"Will you come?" Alya asked. "I'm feared they'll kill Mam and Suli next."

"I'll come," he told her. "But I need you to run to the

Temple and fetch the guards. Tell them what happened. Tell them more people may die if they don't come with everyone they have."

She nodded but didn't move.

"Well, go on then," he said. "I'll look after your mother."

He counted time, watching her run toward the Temple.

I'm ready, said Warrior in his head. Karsman could feel the combat persona's eagerness to take control. He pushed him back firmly.

Not yet.

He took his time getting ready and then walked slowly across the Road to Dijah's shebeen. His best bet was to draw this out as long as he could, giving the Temple guards time to get there. If the fight did escalate, the Temple guards might not stand much of a chance against the soldiers, but at least they would serve as a distraction. And perhaps the soldiers would hesitate to challenge a recognizable civil authority. Perhaps.

When he pushed open the door of Dijah's, one look told him that Alya had been right. Doro was still breathing, but Karsman had seen enough critically injured men to know that he did not have long to live. He lay on the floor with his back against the wall, his head at an unnatural angle, eyes unfocused. His chest rose and fell unevenly as he struggled for breath. A trickle of blood ran down from one nostril and his face was very pale.

Karsman felt a surge of anger. It was not that he liked Doro. No one liked Doro. The man was a bad drunk and a bully. Karsman had been forced to fight him more than once, and it was never a pleasure. Doro fought dirty and never seemed to know when he was beaten. He felt a fleeting relief that he would never have to fight Doro again, then immediately felt guilty for thinking it.

But Doro was one of his people. In an odd way, Karsman felt no less responsible for him than he would for any of the others.

He forced himself to look at the dying man, feeling sick. He had known that sooner or later the townspeople and the soldiers would clash, but he had hidden his head and hoped that the problem would go away. Now Doro was dead and it was Karsman's fault.

The three soldiers stood in a loose group by the bar. There were a surprising number of empty bottles on the table closest to them, but Karsman could tell they were not drunk. They measured him with their eyes, watching to see what he would do.

He looked slowly around the room, evaluating the scene. Behind the bar Dijah and her older daughter were still frozen in shock. As far as he could tell, neither was hurt. The other drinkers had retreated to the far end of the room. Some of the bolder ones had their fists clenched, but none of them made a move toward the soldiers. Karsman dismissed them from his thoughts. A few might join the fight, but only when it was clear which way it would go. If the soldiers got the upper hand, they would stand back and watch him get pounded.

I don't know if we can take all three, said Warrior, sounding unusually cautious.

We're not going to, Karsman told him.

"Is there a problem, big man?" the long-haired soldier asked him. His voice was neutral, but there was no mistaking the threat.

"What happened here?" Karsman asked.

The soldier gestured to the dying man on the floor.

"Your friend attacked me," he said. "Came at me with a knife." He held out his hand palm-up to show Karsman a chisel that he must have taken from Doro.

Karsman had little doubt that Doro had been the aggressor, but he also suspected that he had been provoked. The whole thing reeked of a setup. Assuming it wasn't simply casual sadism, there must be a plan behind it.

They're trying to identify the power relations, said a voice in his head. Stage an incident, then see who steps up to confront them, who everyone else defers to. Congratulations, you've just been made.

So what do I do now?

The same thing that you are already doing, said Strategist. Defer, defuse, deflect. They are looking for anyone who might be a threat to them. If you take them on directly, they will cut you down.

Thanks for nothing, Karsman thought. I could have worked that out for myself.

"What's your name?" he asked the soldier.

The man blinked, as if surprised by the question.

"Flet," he said. "And yours?"

"Karsman."

"So," the soldier said. "Do we have a problem, Mr. Karsman?"

"Not with me," Karsman answered. "But you'll have to explain yourself to the Muljaddy."

The soldier performed a quick little motion with his hand, flipping Doro's chisel from one finger to the next. He brought it down point first on the bar, left it quivering in the plastic surface.

"And where do I find this Muljaddy?"

"Their guards are probably on their way here already."

The door of the shebeen opened as if on cue. The Temple guards showed signs of having been turned out hastily, armor jackets thrown over their black half-dress uniforms. Karsman was relieved to see that the patrol was led by Curinn, the older and more cautious of the two guard captains. He was also glad to see that only Curinn carried a pistol. It was no part of his plan to start a fire-fight in the crowded shebeen.

Flet smiled. "How convenient."

Curinn looked around the room, taking in the standoff and the dying man on the floor. Behind him, his men fanned out in a half circle, hands gripping the butts of their holstered shocksticks.

"Karsman, what's happening here?" Curinn asked.

"Fight," said Karsman. "Between Doro and this . . . visitor."

Curinn looked again at the dying man. He gave Karsman a look that promised nothing good. Now that Karsman had made the incident his problem, he would make sure to repay the favor.

"Who started it?" he asked.

"He attacked me," said Flet. "I defended myself."

"Is this true?" Curinn said, looking around the room. A few of the drinkers nodded. "Karsman?"

"I didn't see the fight," said Karsman. "It was all over by the time I arrived."

On the floor, Doro made a snoring noise. His head tipped forward onto his chest but his eyes remained open, now focused on nothing at all. Curinn looked down at the body and came to a decision.

"You three," he said. "Come with me."

Now, Warrior said.

Karsman let his own consciousness recede, allowing the other persona to expand to fill his brain. He held on to just a thread of control, enough to block Warrior if he tried to move too soon. He shifted his weight imperceptibly, ready for a first strike.

The soldier smiled again. "Of course," he said. He lifted his glass from the bar, and Warrior tensed. Instead of attacking, however, Flet simply drained off the finger of liquor left in it, made a face, and set it back down on the bar. He nodded to his two companions and started to walk toward the door. The half circle of Temple guards opened to let them pass, then closed behind them again.

The fragment of consciousness that was still Karsman reasserted control. Warrior resisted for a moment and then yielded. Karsman put his hand against the doorpost to steady himself, waiting for the moment of dizziness to pass.

On the Road, the guards flanked the three soldiers in a double line. As Karsman watched, Flet turned and looked back at him. He nodded to Karsman and then looked away again.

That went well, said Strategist.

Karsman said nothing. He could not shake the feeling that something had happened he did not understand.

———

When Karsman awoke in his shack the next day it was still early. He slid the blackout shutters on the window open a crack and peered out. The Road was empty and all the shacks that he could see were still shuttered and dark. For the rest, the view was the same as ever. The bloated orange disc of the sun hung in the same part of the sky that it always did, casting its muted light over everything. On either side of the road, the gray towers stood like silent sentinels, their outlines softened by the perpetual haze. Nothing moved.

He looked at the clock by the head of his bed. The glowing wedge marking the time showed it was a little before Morning 6. That was earlier than he usually rose, but he was awake now and he knew that there would be no going back to sleep. He shook his head. It had been after Morning 1 when he had gone to bed, which meant that he had slept less than five hours. Oddly, he felt as if he had been asleep for much longer, and he was intensely hungry.

He pulled himself reluctantly out of bed and splashed some cold water from the demijohn in the kitchen over his face. He thought about taking some of the better pieces of salvage he had gathered over the past week down to the Temple and cashing them in. Then he remembered that Kido's was no longer serving food or drink, so he would have nothing to spend the money on.

For the time being, the Temple and its rituals were his only option if he wanted to eat.

He put on his coveralls and jacket and walked slowly toward the Temple, passing in and out of the permanent shadow cast by the buildings on either side of the Road. The wind had picked up while he was dressing, blowing red dust and scraps of dried plant matter from sun to dark and making the prayer flags stretched between the towers snap and ripple. He pulled his goggles down over his eyes and hunched his shoulders against the gusts.

He was still a little ways from the Temple when he heard the first notes of the early service, rebroadcast by the speakers mounted on the four corner towers. The music this morning was more strident than the hymns to Arinna of the day before, with a martial quality to it. He recognized the opening bars of the dawn hymn to Sabava.

He stopped, frowning. It could not be Sabava's day. Yesterday's service had been dedicated to Arinna. Normally, Teshub followed Arinna, and Sabava followed Teshub. That was how it had been for as long as Karsman had been alive. That was how, if the Muljaddy were to be believed, it had always been.

Had he remembered it wrongly? Perhaps it had been two days ago that he had gone to the Temple to earn his day's food by turning the prayer wheel. But then how would he have eaten yesterday?

He wondered if he was simply confused. He might have mixed up his memories of the service that he had heard. In the shock of Doro's violent death and the face-off with the strangers, maybe he had lost track of time and run the days together.

Or perhaps, exceptionally, the Muljaddy had authorized a change in the order of the services. Rarely—very rarely—the otherwise immutable order of services could be changed. During a Passing, for example, prayers might be offered to Rundas, the god of new beginnings. In times of emergency, two days might be switched so as to dedicate a day of prayers to a particular deity. A day of prayers to Sabava, the most martial of the deities, would make sense if the town was threatened by bandits. Or—an unpleasant thought—it could be intended as a gesture of respect to the visitors. Karsman did not like the idea of that. If it were true, it would mean that the alien soldiers were being treated as honored guests. That did not bode well.

As he stood in the center of the Road and listened to the swelling strains of the hymn, a third explanation occurred to him. Despite the warm wind, he felt himself grow suddenly cold.

He had not mixed up the days. Doro had indeed died on Arinna's day. Today was Sabava's day. There had been no change in the order of worship. He had slept for an entire day, right through the day normally dedicated to Teshub.

At least, he hoped that he had slept.

———————

Was it one of you? Karsman asked.

His personas remained resolutely silent. Karsman was not surprised. Some of them could become positively garrulous whenever anything related to their specialty came up, but they seldom responded to more general questions.

I never wanted any of you, Karsman reminded them. I never asked for this.

He sat down with his back against the metal wall of a building. As always, the surface was cool to the touch, a few degrees below ambient temperature. It was just one of the curious things about the Builder structures. So long as they were intact, they were always a little cooler than the air around them. Strip off a piece, however, and it quickly warmed to the temperature of its surroundings. Sometimes the city seemed to Karsman less like an artificial construct than a living organism, with all its parts interlinked in some manner too subtle to understand.

To his left and right, the Road stretched away, a broad

black line pointed at the horizon. Follow the Road in either direction, and you'd eventually come back to where you started, assuming you didn't starve to death first. But before you reached your starting point, you'd pass through the capital, the largest human-built city on the planet and the home of the Muljaddy family.

Karsman had grown up in the capital. When he was still in his teens, his parents found a place for him as a servant to a Muljaddy. Not a minor provincial Muljaddy living in semi-exile in an isolated Temple along the Road, but a member of the inner family with a palace-tower of her own and a permanent staff of more than a hundred servants and retainers. She also had friends in high places. A few years after Karsman entered her service, she embarked on a tour of twelve neighboring worlds under the auspices of a friendly Intelligence. A handful of chosen staff accompanied her. Karsman was one of them.

For the first six stops of the tour, his duties consisted of little more than looking smart in a uniform and running minor errands for the Muljaddy and the more senior servants. Then, abruptly, everything changed. The sponsoring Intelligence's priorities shifted and it lost interest in its erstwhile protégée. The scheduled onward trip was canceled and the travelers were left stranded on an unfamiliar world. Lines of credit dried up. The Muljaddy, for the first time in her life, was threatened not just with poverty but irrelevance. Far from home on an unfamiliar star world, the fact that her family were absolute rulers of a backwater cut no ice at all.

The Muljaddy improvised. Spending the credit still available to her, she bought her way into a new network of patronage ultimately backed by a different tribe of Intelligences. With the help of her new friends, she mapped a route home. The only problem was that the new offer was open to at most three people. To get home at all, the Muljaddy would need to abandon most of her entourage, including her guards and her ladies-in-waiting.

To his surprise, Karsman was not among those abandoned. A Muljaddy of her rank could not travel without an entourage to serve and protect her, to smooth the obstacles in her path and negotiate on her behalf. If she was allowed only two retainers, then those two retainers would have to fulfill all the required roles.

No one asked Karsman for his consent. The Muljaddy made another deal, and people he had never seen before came to take him to a hospital, where he obediently allowed himself to be scanned and probed and subjected to a long series of tests. When all the tests were finished, they led him to a tiny waiting room and gave him a paper cup of orange liquid to drink. His last thought was that the liquid was unpleasantly sweet. Then all his thoughts went away.

He had had basic modification surgery when he first left home, to give him a greater tolerance for conditions on other worlds. What the surgeons did to him now was far more radical and invasive. While he slept, they remapped the structure of his brain, splicing in artificial neural complexes that gave him the ability to play host to a dozen or more different personas. Each one was a specialist, a constructed personality that was less than completely human but that compensated for its limitations with a profound knowledge of some useful skill. To make room for the new personas, they took away most of his memories from his childhood, a certain amount of his learning ability, and a large part of his own identity.

When he went to sleep, he was a callow boy from a backwater world with no particular talents beyond a strong back and the willingness to make himself useful. When he woke again, he found himself sharing his mind with a crowd of experts.

It took five months to get home again, five months in which Karsman acted as the Muljaddy's bodyguard and facilitator, interpreter and manservant. Assisted by the remaining maid, he cooked and cleaned and helped the Muljaddy dress for formal occasions. If she sometimes required more personal services from her servants, Karsman had no memory of them afterward. Discretion was part of the guarantee.

When they reached home at last, Karsman waited a week. Then he ran, without really knowing what he was running from. He slipped out of the palace early one morning and hitched a ride on a road train. For the next three months, he begged lifts and did odd jobs, working his way along the Road, farther and farther from the capital. In the confusion of a Passing Festival, he changed his name and joined a new Temple. By the time the Temple's Muljaddy finally ordered a halt in an almost pristine Builder city stuck between a belt of sun swamps and a range of dry hills, more than four thousand kilometers of Road lay between Karsman and his birthplace.

If his sometime mistress ever looked for her lost investment, Karsman never heard about it. He kept his head down and did his best to blend in. He never told anyone about the personas. As the years went by, he started to believe that he had left his past behind him.

Now, all of a sudden, he was not so sure anymore.

"Different how?" asked Steck. He and Karsman were huddled in the lee of the tower where Steck had been working, sheltered from the worst of the wind that blew across the Road from the swamps to sunward.

"Did I do anything unusual? Say anything out of character?"

Steck shrugged. "I wasn't with you most of the day. When I was, I guess you were a little quieter than usual. But you've been quiet a lot lately. I assumed it had something to do with that girl from the Festival." He used his knife to scrape caked-on carbon from the muzzle of his cutting torch. "I'm glad you didn't go with her in the end. The place would be dull without you."

"Dull is not exactly our problem at the moment," Karsman said.

"True that," agreed Steck. "What do you think the Muljaddy has done with those guys?"

"No idea. I hoped the guards would just kick them out of town. But I don't think they're ready to leave yet. If the guards had tried anything, we'd probably have heard the fight from here."

No one had seen the three strangers since the night of Doro's murder. If the Muljaddy had sent them away or thrown them in one of the holding cells under the Temple, they must have submitted quietly. There had been no evidence of a fight in the vicinity of the Temple. But in any case, Karsman doubted that even a full squad of Temple guards would be able to make the strangers do anything they did not want to do.

A little distance from where Steck and Karsman were sitting, a crew was working in one of the nearby ruins. Kars-man watched them carrying thin sheets of flexible metal out of the building. He looked up and down the Road, at the vast towers that rose on either side of it, their tops wreathed in perpetual halos of pale mist. Ten years of work by the people of the strip-town, industriously prying free any loose materials they could find, had little more than scratched the surface of the city. You could easily take the buildings for untouched, unaltered from the day that they had been built by whatever godlike Intelligences had created the Road and all the enigmatic cities along it.

"Why did you ask me if you had done anything differ-ent?" Steck asked.

"No real reason."

It was no longer possible for Karsman to deny what had happened. He had been gone, completely submerged, for the whole of the previous day. To judge by the way he felt now, he must have been up part of the night as well. One of his personas had taken over, taken over so completely that he had no memory at all of the events of the day before.

He no idea which persona it had been. His first fear was that it had been Warrior. But if Warrior had taken over, there would be traces of violence. He had searched his body for cuts and bruises and found none. As far as he could tell, there were no dead bodies lying around.

But if not Warrior, then who?

CHAPTER FOUR

Kido's was still dark and silent the next morning when Karsman got up. Apparently the soldiers' threats had been enough to frighten the shopkeeper into staying closed.

His stomach growled. He had always preferred to buy most of his food and water from Kido's, accepting the Muljaddy's dole as little as possible. In practice that translated to two or three days of mandatory worship every nine-day, and six or seven days eating provisions that he bought with scrip issued in return for salvaged materials. All the food ultimately came from the Muljaddy's food processors, but at least buying it from Kido spared him having to act out the rituals of a religion that meant nothing to him.

Now, however, he had no option. His own supplies were almost exhausted. If he wanted to eat today, he would have to play by the Muljaddy's rules.

Before he reached the Temple, however, he realized something strange was happening.

The Temple sat a little ways from the end of the strip-town on a plot of its own, surrounded by a decorative fence marking the boundary between the sacred and the profane. Normally, the gate to the Road stood open, allowing free access to the Temple. Today it was closed, and a small detachment of Temple guards stood beside the gate, hands on their weapons. A crowd had gathered outside the fence, keeping their distance but not showing any inclination to disperse. The crowd, Karsman saw, was mostly made up of men.

"They won't let us in," someone told Karsman as he pushed his way to the front. "They say only women can go in now."

Karsman was not surprised to see that the officer in charge of the guards was Magnan, the younger of the two captains. Karsman and Curinn might have a grudging respect for each other, but Magnan was another matter. He was a bully by nature, quick to insist on the cringing obedience that he seemed to feel was his due. He had a particular dislike for Karsman, who he clearly saw as a permanent challenge to his authority. Naturally, if anything ugly was happening, Magnan would be in the middle of it.

"Come on," Magnan called out to one of the women who hovered uncertainly at the front of the crowd. "Or are you planning to hang around out there all day?"

The woman's husband pulled at her arm. "Don't go in

there, Nisa," he told her. "Either they let us in together or we don't go in."

"What are you doing?" Karsman asked.

Magnan looked at him, a sneer on his face. "Mind your business," he said. "Mind your business and wait your turn. Women first. Men after."

"Since when do we have turns?" Karsman said.

"Since the Muljaddy ordered it," said Magnan.

A man standing behind Karsman tugged at his sleeve.

"My wife's in there. And my daughter," he said.

"Your wife and daughter are perfectly safe," Magnan told the man, raising his voice slightly. "Now, the rest of you women, come forward. You want to go in and pray and eat, go in now. Or you can wait here and stay hungry. You choose."

"We've never done things this way before," Karsman told him.

Magnan put his hands on the hips of his fatigues.

"Well, this is how we do things now," he said. "And this is how it's going to be for as long as the Muljaddy wants it. Clear?"

Karsman was conscious of the eyes of the men around him. He could feel them willing him to do what they were afraid to do. He knew that if he backed down now his reputation would never be the same again. He could still turn his back and walk away, but it would make things harder in the future.

He sighed. "I'm going in now."

"I said, women only."

"And I said I'm going in."

The two men faced each other. Magnan was nearly a head shorter than Karsman, but he was armed and Karsman was not. He slowly lowered his hand until it was resting on the butt of his pistol. Behind him, the other guards gripped their shocksticks more tightly.

Let me take him, said Warrior. We can take all of them.

Karsman fought the temptation to let Warrior take control. He met Magnan's eyes, not challenging, but simply asserting himself.

At last, Magnan stepped to one side.

"Go in if you want, Karsman," he said. The sneer was still there.

———————

Walking across the Temple compound, Karsman expected at any moment to hear Magnan give the order to fire, to feel the burn of bullets in his back. With a great effort, he slowed his pace, doing his best to appear nonchalant.

Neither the order nor the bullets ever came. He reached the steps of the Temple and began to climb, setting one foot deliberately after the other. He looked straight ahead, careful not to make eye contact with the guards on either side of the door. Calm, he told himself. It's all right. Magnan said you could go in.

Instead of taking the stairs to the side corridor with the prayer wheels, he walked down the broad ramp that led down into the main hall. The large space was close to half full, with more than two hundred women and girls inside, watched over by the Muljaddy's guards and a couple of priests. Karsman caught the eye of the woman closest to him and read fear on her face.

Give me control, Warrior insisted.

Not yet, said Karsman.

The far end of the prayer hall was dominated by a raised dais on which stood the altar and statues of all nine gods. The Muljaddy was sitting on a throne to the right of the altar, their white robes glowing brilliantly in the light of a single spotlight, cowl drawn down to conceal their face. Next to them stood the giant soldier, watching over the crowd from behind his black visor, his arms folded across his huge chest. Karsman saw that he now wore a pistol in a holster at his hip.

One of the other soldiers, the man named Flet, stood just in front of the dais. As Karsman watched, two Temple guards led one of the women to him. When they released her arms, she stood motionless, as if paralyzed by fear.

The soldier reached out and took her hand. With surprising gentleness, he guided her fingers to touch a small tablet that he held. After a moment, he let go of her hand and raised the tablet so that it was level with her eyes, held it there for a few seconds, and then lowered it again and spent a few moments studying whatever it displayed. Finally, he nodded. The guards led the woman over to join a group of women squatting by the wall. As she crouched down beside them, a second pair of guards was already pulling another woman from the crowd and leading her toward the dais.

The process repeated. The second woman was dismissed, and a third was led forward, followed by a fourth and then a fifth. The soldier worked quietly and methodically, inspecting each in turn, pausing sometimes for as much as a minute to review the results of each scan. His manner was casual and unhurried. If not for the military cut of his clothing and the gun by his side, Karsman might almost have taken him for a doctor and the black-uniformed guards for his orderlies. Only the look of fear on the faces of the women awaiting screening said plainly that something very different was happening.

And what happens, Karsman wondered, if he finds the one he's looking for? He looked toward the giant on the dais and saw how the man tensed almost imperceptibly as each woman was led forward. Karsman guessed that the big soldier had been appointed the executioner. He could see how it would play out: the slightest signal from Flet and the big man would move in, bringing the whole business to a quick, bloody conclusion. And Karsman would be powerless to do anything to prevent it.

"Enjoying the show?" said a soft voice at Karsman's side. Karsman turned to find the third soldier standing barely an arm's length from him. The man had approached him so quietly that even Warrior had not registered his presence until an instant before he spoke.

"What are you doing?" Karsman asked.

"Looking for someone," the man said. His voice was low and there was something about his manner that could almost have been mistaken for timidity.

"Who?"

"Just a woman."

"One of these women?" Karsman asked.

The soldier shrugged. "Maybe," he said.

"And when you find her?" Karsman asked him.

"We kill her. And then we go home."

"And if she's not among them?"

"Then we look for her among the rest of the women in town." He gestured around him. "They all have to come here eventually if they want to eat."

"And if you still don't find her? What if she's not here?" Karsman persisted.

"Then we wait. Sooner or later, she has to come."

Karsman looked at the frightened crowd in the center of the hall. "Who is she?" he asked. "Why do you want to kill her?"

The mercenary looked at him directly. "Who she is is none of your business," he said. "And neither is 'why.'"

He put his hand on Karsman's arm, and it took all of Karsman's willpower to hold Warrior in check.

"Don't get involved," the soldier told him. "This isn't anything to do with you." He released his hold. "Now go. You and the rest of the men can come back later, when we're done."

Karsman thought about letting Warrior loose. He thought that with the advantage of surprise he could probably kill or disable the smaller man. But that would leave him with the two other soldiers and most of the Muljaddy's guards to deal with. The balance of force was overwhelmingly against him. Unarmed, without even the advantage of surprise, he could not hope to win.

"Go," the soldier repeated. This time Karsman obeyed. He climbed the ramp slowly, conscious of the soldier watching him. Inside him, Warrior seethed with impatience.

At the entrance to the Temple compound, the crowd was waiting to hear what he had to say.

"Tell them," said Magnan.

"The women are inside. They have not been harmed," Karsman said. The people in the crowd stared at him, sullen and uncomprehending.

"You heard what he said," Magnan told the crowd. "Now get out of here, all of you. We'll let you know when you can come back."

Karsman took a step toward the gate, but Magnan held up his hand. "Not you, Karsman. I'm not done with you." He made a gesture, and the guards who had stepped back to let Karsman pass closed in around him.

"You should show more respect," Magnan said. "So it's time we taught you a lesson."

The guards moved closer, drawing their shocksticks from their belts.

———

Karsman sat beside Kido's store, leaning forward slightly to keep the bruises on his back clear of the wall of the store. He dabbed at his cut lip, wincing as his fingers touched the tender flesh. The guards had continued to beat him after he had fallen, raining blows across his back and his arms and legs. At least they had not used the shock function of their sticks. Being shocked was worse than any ordinary beating.

From where he sat, he could see more Temple guards

moving along the line of shacks that made up the strip-town, pushing open doors and looking in windows. Apparently the strangers were not content to simply sit and wait for their victim to come to them after all.

We should stop them, said Warrior. Karsman paid the persona no attention. It had taken all his strength to hold Warrior back when the guards were beating him. Warrior was designed for offense, not for peaceful resistance. A beating was an attack, to be answered with equal or superior force. The notion that there might be times when you had to lie down and take a beating was outside Warrior's way of thinking.

He wondered if Strategist had a plan that would let him defeat his adversaries, but the persona had gone deep, barely responding. Karsman could still feel him there, lurking in the back of his mind, but he showed no inclination to be foregrounded. Was it possible for a persona to feel embarrassed? Perhaps Strategist was unwilling to admit that he had no more idea than Karsman how to deal with the situation.

He brushed at the crust of drying blood on his lip and saw a fresh dark smear across his fingertips. He shook his head. The beating did not matter. He had had worse beatings from the Temple guards before. What mattered was that the Muljaddy had thrown in with the outsiders. Karsman had harbored some vague plans of his own of using the power of the Temple against the strangers. Now it seemed that they were working together.

———

"You look like hell," said Steck.

"It's not as bad as it looks," said Karsman.

I was asking for it, he thought to himself. Serves me right for always trying to take up everyone's causes.

That sounds very noble, sneered Strategist, but we both know that it's pride. You always want to be the big man who everyone looks up to. One day that will get you killed.

When did you become the voice of my conscience? Karsman asked.

Oh, I just don't want you screwing up my long-term plans with your poorly thought-out heroics, Strategist said.

You have long-term plans? Do tell.

Strategist did not answer, and Karsman felt the persona retreat again, withdrawing into the background of Karsman's mind to sleep or scheme. Strategist was hard to like. Warrior's homicidal eagerness might be more likely to get Karsman into trouble, but Strategist's arrogance and perpetual pose of superiority made him harder to live with.

There was a shout from the far side of the road and a brief scuffle by one of the shacks, abruptly terminated by the electric buzz of a shockstick. Karsman and Steck watched a group of black-uniformed Temple guards wrestle someone to the ground.

"That's Tofik's house," said Steck. He looked at Karsman expectantly. Karsman shook his head. The two watched in silence as some of the guards pulled Tofik away, his body twitching and his feet dragging in the dirt. Others forced open the door of Tofik's shack and went inside.

"Things are getting crazy," Steck observed.

"Yes," said Karsman.

"I don't mean this." Steck gestured to the guards leading Tofik's wife and daughters from his shack, while others held back a sullen crowd of onlookers with their sticks. "I mean the other stuff."

"Such as?"

"The city's changing," said Steck. "Haven't you noticed?"

Karsman looked at the gray towers that loomed over them. As far as he could tell, they looked the same as ever.

"That tower there—Sixteen," said Steck. "It was always shorter than the Twins. Now look at it."

Karsman frowned. The skyline of the city was so familiar that he had long ago ceased to pay any attention to it. Yet now that he thought about it, Steck might be right. The flattened rhomboid of the tower seemed more elongated than he remembered, and the stubby spire that crowned it now definitely rose above the tops of its neighbors. Near the top were a cluster of projecting vanes that seemed unfamiliar.

"Twenty-Four's changed, too. I've been working on a piece up there. When I came back yesterday morning it had rotated a quarter-turn to the right. Some of the others are showing new lights, but Three and Six have gone dark." Steck gestured toward the tops of the tallest buildings. "Even the mist up there is different," he said.

"In what way?"

"I don't know. Just . . . different." He hesitated. "Do you think the soldiers are doing this?"

"Maybe," said Karsman. It seemed reasonable. The city had been stable for as long as he could remember. If it had begun to change now, just as the soldiers arrived, it was probably not a coincidence.

"Do you think they're Builders?" Steck asked.

Karsman considered the idea. The Builders were always thought of as godlike beings, remote and inscrutable. All anyone knew of them was that they had made the Road and the cities and then, so far as anyone could tell, vanished utterly.

Popular belief was full of theories about them, of course. Some people thought the Builders were the servants of the Nine Gods and that the cities were palaces built for the deities. But if that were the case, then taking apart the towers for scrap would be sacrilege of the most heinous kind. Given that the Muljaddy actually encouraged people to scavenge the ruins, that couldn't be the case. Maybe the Builders were not servants but enemies of the gods. The matter remained a mystery. The Muljaddy themselves had declined, as far as Karsman knew, to issue any unambiguous declaration on the subject.

As a child, Karsman had never worried too much about the details. Later, when he traveled off-world, he learned that the universe was filled with cooperating or competing Powers. Powers were of many different kinds: post-humans, the evolved artificial minds known as Intelligences, and strange hybrids of the two. Even if they weren't gods in the strictest sense of the word, they possessed abilities that far surpassed those of mere humans. Clearly, the Builders must have been such a Power.

If so, they were simply one among many. No one Karsman met could tell him who the Builders really were or why they had made the Road, but the galaxy turned out to be littered with artifacts made by one faction or another. The Road was just one more. For all Karsman knew, it might have been something that the Builders had thrown together in the same way a man might put up a plastic-board shack, slotting the prefabricated pieces together to have somewhere to sleep for a few nights and then abandoning it without a second thought when it was no longer needed.

He did not talk about any of this with his neighbors. Even Steck, to whom Karsman had confided a little about his past, had struggled with the idea that the universe was home not to nine gods but to nine thousand or more. In any case, the distinction between an actual god and a being that merely possessed godlike powers was too subtle for him. If an Intelligence could fly between stars as quick as thought, conjure up vast structures, and create whole races of novel living things to do its work, even reshape whole planets, who was Karsman to say that it wasn't really a god? After a while, Karsman gave up trying to argue the finer points and just let the matter rest.

"No," Karsman told Steck at last. "I don't think they're Builders."

He could not say for certain why he thought so, but he was sure that he was right. For all their arrogance, there was something furtive about the soldiers. If the Builders came back to reclaim what they had made, everyone would know.

Three men isn't a return in force, observed Warrior. It isn't even an invading army. Three men is a commando unit. Whoever they are, whoever they're working for, they're operating behind enemy lines.

CHAPTER FIVE

The Temple guards came down the line of the strip-town again early the next day, banging on doors and turning people out into the wind. Karsman came out of his shack to find his neighbors, some only half dressed, being pushed and chivvied into lines by squads of guards who looked almost as ill-tempered as they did.

"What the hell's going on?" he asked the man closest to him.

The man shook his head, one hand held over his eyes to protect them from windblown dust. The guards had turned him out of his home without even giving him time to put on his goggles. "More trouble from those damned off-worlders," he said. He cleared his throat and spat a mouthful of red dust on the ground at his feet.

"Go get your mask and jacket," Karsman said.

"But the guards—"

"Get them. I'll cover for you."

A flat-truck rolled past. An amplified voice boomed from the cab. "—groups of ten. Anyone who isn't at the Temple in five doesn't eat today. Leave your tools behind—you won't need them. Form into groups of ten—"

It took the guards more than an hour to round up the last of the stragglers, an hour in which the rest of the people of the strip-town stood and grumbled outside the closed gate of the Temple precinct. The wind was warm but fierce, raising streamers of red dust from the dry ground. People huddled in small groups, their heads bowed and shoulders hunched against the blast. Karsman was relieved to see that men and women were once again mingled together. Apparently the soldiers' project of separating the sexes had been only temporary. He wondered if they had already found the woman they were looking for and, if so, whether they had killed her. No one around him seemed to know.

A little after Morning 8, the great doors at the rear of the Temple opened and the three soldiers emerged. There was no sign of the Muljaddy or its priests. Karsman watched as the three men took up position on the steps, Flet in the middle, the other two standing a few paces behind him on either side. All three wore sidearms openly now.

"Now, listen up," said Flet. His voice boomed from the speakers mounted on the towers of the Temple. "In a few minutes, we're going to open the doors. The guards will let you in, ten at a time. Pick up your food, then come back outside. When you're outside, stay with your group. Everyone understand?"

"What about the service?" someone asked.

"No service today," Flet said. The announcement caused a ripple of consternation in the crowd. Flet stood with his hands on his hips for a moment, as if assessing the mood of the crowd. "Listen up," he said again. "New rules. From now on, if you want to eat, you work. Real work. No more turning wheels and muttering prayers. You want a day's food, you do a day's work. Everyone understand?"

A woman in the crowd called out something in which Karsman only caught the word "children."

"Children too young to work eat for free," Flet said. "Children old enough to work earn their food same as everyone else. Got it?"

There was a sullen murmur from the crowd. A few of the men closest to the Temple steps started to move forward, but the guards took a step toward them, holding their shocksticks in front of them, and the men fell back.

"What kind of work?" called a voice from the crowd.

Flet turned toward the speaker.

"To begin with," he said, "we're going to move the Temple."

It had been twelve years since the Temple had last moved under its own power. Sand and dust had piled up in deep drifts around its eighteen giant wheels. Tangles of wind-blown weeds and brush fouled the massive axles.

Karsman spent most of the morning working to help dig out one of the wheels and clear away the caked-on laterite deposits clinging to the understructure. By the end of the morning, his back ached from stooping and he had skinned his knuckles almost to the bone on a projecting piece of the motor assembly. If it had not been for the fact that all three soldiers were now visibly armed, he might have added his voice to the sullenly militant faction among the men who were in favor of finishing with the off-worlders once and for all.

At noon, a Temple guard told his group to take a break and collect their midday meal from inside the Temple. When Karsman emerged from the trench where he had been working, he saw that more than half of the great structure had already been dug free. Workers crawled over the sides of the Temple, and a double line of men and women carried buckets of sand and soil away from the site to empty them in the desert.

The interior of the Temple was dark. The stairway to the upper level had been closed off, and the main hall was empty and silent. In the gloom, the statues of the gods glimmered dully, lit only by threads of light that filtered in from the narrow skylights set in the roof of the hall. Even the incense that normally filled the inner spaces of the Temple had faded to almost nothing, replaced by the acrid smell of dust and the musty odor of the distant swamps. There was no sign of the Muljaddy or the priests.

Despite his atheism, Karsman felt a pang of loss. He might not believe in the Muljaddy's gods, but he liked the peaceful familiarity of the rituals, the sonority of the music and the sermons. The new regime imposed by the soldiers made no attempt to disguise autocracy with the pageantry of religion, but it was no more democratic for that. When it came down to it, Karsman found little reason to prefer the rule of the gun to the rule of the gods.

As he was making his way outside again, holding a plastic tub of noodles in broth and a squeeze bottle of water, someone called his name. He turned and saw that it was the smallest of the three soldiers, the man who had spoken to him in the Temple the day before.

"You're Karsman, right?" the soldier said.

Karsman nodded.

"They tell me you're a mechanic. I need something built. Can you do that for me?"

"Depends what it is," Karsman said.

The soldier beckoned. "Come with me."

———————

"How much power is this supposed to carry again?" Karsman said.

"You think you can't do it?" the soldier said.

"Give me the materials and I can build the coupling. Whether it will hold up is another question."

They were squatting in a narrow recess at the base of one of the towers, a recess that only moments before had been hidden behind an access panel that Karsman would never even have known was there. From the back wall of the recess protruded a device that the soldier claimed was a power connector. If so, it was bigger than any Karsman had ever seen. He wondered what the soldiers planned to hook up to it.

"It doesn't need to last forever," the soldier said. "The facility is self-powering. It just needs a kick to get it going."

"The facility?"

The soldier made a circular motion with his hand to indicate the city around them.

"The city?" said Karsman.

"This one and all the others."

Karsman was silent for a moment, absorbing the idea. It had never occurred to him before that all the cities along the Road could be part of an interconnected whole.

"What is it?" he asked.

"An Intelligence," the soldier said. "Or it was once. And could be again." He turned his head slightly to look at Karsman's face. "You know what an Intelligence is," he said.

"Yes," said Karsman.

"Interesting." His eyes narrowed slightly. "What's your story? You're not like the others." He shifted his balance slightly as he spoke. Even without Warrior to point it out for him Karsman recognized the implicit threat in the movement. He was suddenly aware of the way that the cramped recess limited his own freedom of movement. He stared straight ahead, careful not to let his eyes stray to the weapon on the soldier's hip.

"I lived in the capital," he said. "I worked for a Muljaddy there."

"Ah," the soldier said. He relaxed, apparently satisfied by the explanation.

"So what are you planning to do?" Karsman asked.

The soldier shook his head. "Don't get curious," he said. "Remember what I told you before."

"Don't get involved," said Karsman.

"That's right." He stood up. "Come on, let's get you to work. You'll find the parts and tools you need in the Temple."

CHAPTER SIX

Karsman was dreaming. In his dream, the loose panel on the side of his shack, the one that always banged when the wind picked up, had finally torn away completely, opening it up to the elements. He could feel the wind blowing across him as he lay in bed, covering him with its payload of fine sand. The sun shone through the opening, bathing the interior with orange light. He squeezed his eyes closed, trying to shut it out.

You have to get up, said a voice in his head.

The voice pulled him out of the dream, but he did not open his eyes. He lay still, feeling the hard surface of his bed under him, the fine grit on his skin.

He became aware that he was still wearing his jacket and coveralls. He must have been so tired the night before that he had fallen into bed without undressing.

Get up, Karsman, said the voice again.

Leave me alone, he told it, and rolled over. Something hard jabbed him in the side.

His eyes flickered open. He pushed himself up on one elbow and looked around him.

At first what he saw made no sense. He lay on a flat gray metal surface, lightly filmed with red dust. Beyond the edge of the metal were layers of color, laid out in diminishing stripes under an orange glow almost too bright to look at.

He pushed himself onto his hands and knees and tried to stand up, but the wind tugged at him and he dropped down again, scrabbling for a handhold on the smooth metal. He pressed himself flat, hardly daring to move.

He lay there for a long moment. Gusts of wind pulled at his jacket. From somewhere above him he heard a dull droning sound that he guessed must be a length of wire or thin metal vibrating in the wind. He closed his eyes, slowly gathering the courage to push himself up and roll over into a sitting position.

The roof of the tower on which he was sitting was a flattened pyramid crowned by a stubby spire made of a black glassy material. The slope of the roof was very gentle, but there was no parapet or railing around it. On hands and knees, he crawled as close to the edge as he dared and found himself looking directly down onto the Road. On the far side, the shacks and warehouses of the strip-town huddled against the base of other towers, reduced to the size of toys by distance. The Road itself was empty, the doors and windows of the houses firmly shuttered. Fine veils of sand blew across the black surface, forming patterns like red lace that swirled for an instant and then disappeared. Nothing else moved.

He raised his eyes and saw the wide swathe of red desert that stretched to darkward, the red slowly fading to a dull ochre as it receded. A band of white fog hovered above the distant horizon and a rift in the clouds showed an orange sky speckled with points of light.

He crawled back up to the summit of the roof and put one arm around the spire. It was warm to the touch, much warmer than it should have been. He could feel a faint vibration through the soles of his boots.

He rested his head against the spire and closed his eyes again.

The last thing that he remembered, he had been working on the connector that the soldier had wanted. Machining the parts that he needed by hand in the settlement's workshop and then assembling everything under the soldier's direction had taken him two days. It was pleasantly undemanding work, much better than shoveling dirt underneath the Temple. He did it all in a state something like meditation, letting Artificer guide his hands and make all the decisions.

Of all his personas, Artificer was the most unassuming and the least problematic. In some ways, Artificer was not properly a persona at all. He never spoke as the others did. He was more like a state of mind, a state of mind in which Karsman instinctively knew what to do. The solutions to mechanical or electrical problems simply suggested themselves, and Karsman's hands moved smoothly to execute them. Karsman had always had some talent for this type of work, but he would have to admit that most of his reputation as a skilled craftsman he owed to Artificer.

So Karsman had called on Artificer to help him fabricate the connector. But Artificer and Karsman always worked as a team, with Karsman in full control. Artificer had never before seized control the way that Warrior or Diplomat might.

On hands and knees, he crawled back to the edge of the roof and looked down. Below him, the bulk of the Temple was slewed across the Road. A rectangular patch of discolored soil surrounded by a low fence marked the spot where it had stood for the last decade. Great ruts in the earth, strewn with loose stone, showed where it had been dug out. One side of the fence that surrounded it was flattened.

The Temple had been pulled up close to the base of the adjacent tower. A heavy umbilical jutting from its lower part joined it to one of the towers. Karsman could just make out the coupling that he had made attached to one end of the cable. He had no memory of finishing it, but there it was.

As he crouched by the edge of the roof, something below him caught his eye. Three meters below the lip of the roof, a broad ledge ran around the tower, punctuated at intervals by vaned finials that jutted out like a crown. At one corner, a climbing rope had been attached to an eyelet at the base of the finial. Karsman almost smiled. He might not have any idea how he got up onto the roof, but he had at least found a way down.

He made a last survey of the roof, looking for any hatch or opening that might offer an easier way down. Finding none, he went back to the edge and looked down on the ledge below. The drop to the ledge itself was nothing. What worried Karsman was the continuation of the drop: two hundred meters to the Road below.

If you're scared, give me control, said Warrior's voice in his head.

Stay out of this, said Karsman.

He looked over the edge once more, focusing on the ledge below, and then squatted down. He was tempted to turn his back to the edge, so as not to have to see that vertiginous drop, but the idea of falling backward into the void horrified him. He sat down, leaning back on his hands, and started to inch forward until his feet were at the edge of the roof. Slowly, he slid forward, letting his legs dangle.

He sat on the edge of the roof, legs swinging, hands

pressed flat against the metal on either side of him. Below him was the ledge, ahead of him the corner finial with its whiplike antenna. All he had to do now was push himself off.

He froze. He could not do it.

Give, said Warrior.

No, said Karsman.

There was a moment of no-time. Suddenly, Karsman was standing on the ledge, gripping the finial with both hands.

You pushed me, you fucker, Karsman said.

You'd have been up there all day, Warrior said. I had to do something.

Did you take control before? Karsman asked. Did you make me climb that tower?

Not me, said Warrior. I have better things to do than risk your neck climbing buildings.

Karsman surveyed the ledge. One of the finials bore signs of having been worked on, the metal at the base discolored by the flame of a cutting torch and scored by the marks of tools. He guessed that it was Steck's work; Steck was the undisputed king of high-altitude salvage.

Karsman lacked Steck's fondness for heights, but at least a roped descent held fewer terrors for him. He searched around the ledge until he found Steck's equipment bag tucked away in a niche. Inside he found tools, rope, and a spare climbing harness. He checked it over, taking a few moments to replace one of the carabiners with one that looked a little less rusty. He let out the straps and buckled on the harness.

Into the hands of the gods, he thought to himself as he clipped onto the rope.

You sure you don't want me to do this? Warrior asked.

Shut up, Karsman said.

Descending a tower on a fixed rope was something he could do. He felt a moment of fear as he swung himself over the edge, but after that it was just a matter of going through the motions. He fell into the rhythm of it—push off with both feet, glide down, pause for a second, then push off again, never looking down, keeping his eyes fixed on the gray steel wall an arm's length in front of his face. Secure in his harness, even the buffeting of the wind seemed more playful than threatening.

Then a new worry struck him. Dangling from the tallest tower in the city, he was painfully conspicuous. If one of the soldiers happened to look up and see him descending the tower, he would have a hard time explaining what he was doing up there.

Normally, it would not matter. People worked on the high towers all the time. But today, Karsman had seen no other climbers on the other buildings. In fact, he had seen no one else at all. That struck him as strange. The strip-town was never entirely deserted. People left their homes to work or socialize at any hour under the light of a sun that never set. There should have been at least a few people crossing the Road, walking to the Temple to eat or worship, or simply sitting outside their shacks. Instead, there was no one at all.

The drop to ground level seemed to take forever. By the time his feet finally touched the earth, the muscles of his thighs burned from the strain of pushing off from the tower. He unfastened his harness with shaking fingers, clipped it back onto the line. Let Steck wonder who had been borrowing his equipment. Karsman wasn't about to tell anyone that he had been climbing buildings in the middle of the night, not until he had some better answers himself.

He looked down the Road toward his shack. The emptiness of the Road unnerved him. He imagined snipers stationed on the tops of towers like the one he had just climbed down from. He considered walking on the desert side of the city, keeping the buildings between him and the uncannily silent town.

Not a good idea, commented Warrior.

How so?

They'll have set a perimeter on either side of the city. Screamers, spy-eyes. Maybe micro-mines. Flip guns.

You think so?

It's what I'd do, said Warrior.

So what do I do? asked Karsman.

Take the Road, said Strategist. Shortest distance. Best chance of talking your way out of it if they catch you.

I'm not doing anything wrong, Karsman protested.

Says the man who goes climbing buildings at night, said Strategist.

He was still more than two hundred meters from his shack when two men emerged from between the buildings and started to walk toward him. Karsman knew them at once, the giant soldier by his height, Flet by his loose-limbed way of walking. An image from an ancient piece of media that Karsman had once seen came back to him: men in archaic clothes walking in a desert town, primitive guns in leather pouches by their sides, pacing slowly toward each other before pulling out their guns and shooting each other down. He remembered smoke, and animals screaming, and wounded men thrashing in the dust. But I don't even have a gun, he thought.

Both Flet and the giant had guns, though, and they were drawn and pointed as they approached Karsman. Karsman noticed abstractedly that they were the same model that the Temple guards carried.

"What are you doing out?" Flet asked him. "Is there something about the idea of a curfew that you don't understand?"

"I was finishing some work. On the coupling," said Karsman. "I must have fallen asleep."

The lie sounded flat and unconvincing to him. He looked at each man in turn, doing his best to look unconcerned. When he tried to meet the giant's eyes, he saw only his own face reflected in the man's black glass visor.

Flet's eyes moved slightly, and Karsman guessed that he was communicating with someone. Naturally, the soldiers would all be wired together. They could hardly function as a unit if they were not. He braced himself for the bullet that would end his life.

"Fine," said Flet at last. "You can go."

"Thank you," said Karsman.

Flet held up a hand. "One more thing," he said. "I feel like I'm seeing your face around too much. You might be a big man in this shitpile. You might think that because you've been useful to us you're somehow untouchable. Don't count on it. If you piss me off even slightly, I will shoot you in the head and walk over your body. Do we understand each other?"

"Perfectly," said Karsman.

"Now get out of here. Curfew ends at Morning Seven. Stick your face outside your door before then and I'll put a bullet through it."

For once, all Karsman's personas were silent as he walked away. Even Warrior seemed cowed. Karsman felt a trickle of sweat run down his side.

He was still feeling shaky when he arrived at the door of his shack. He had no clear idea what time it was, but he wanted nothing more than to lie down in his bed and sleep for a week. He reached for the handle.

Wait, said Warrior.

Huh?

The door's open.

Karsman froze. The door was ajar, swaying slightly in the wind. As he watched, it swung inward a few centimeters, then rebounded gently from some unseen obstacle inside. The projecting latch clicked against the doorframe with just too little force to let the door close fully.

He realized that his work knife was in his hand. Warrior was clamoring to be allowed to take control. With an effort, Karsman forced him down.

He put his hand on the door and pushed. There was a moment's resistance before it opened. He pushed the door wider, stepped over an unfamiliar jacket on the floor.

The shack was as he had left it, the only thing out of place an earthenware container that held the last of his provisions. He was sure that he had left it in one of the cabinets, but now it stood empty on the table, its lid beside it.

A soft noise caught his attention and he turned his

gaze to the bed. There was a hunched shape under the blankets, a tuft of lilac hair on the pillow. He took a step into the room.

Mera sat up in bed, blinking in the light.

"Hello, Karsman," she said. "Do you have any more food? I'm starving."

————————

Later, as they lay squeezed together in Karsman's narrow bed, Mera ran her fingers over his cheek.

"I sort of thought that you'd be more glad to see me," she said.

Karsman breathed out slowly. He felt the warmth of her skin against his chest, the pressure of her lean, muscular body against his.

"Of course I'm glad," he said. "It's just that this . . . this isn't the best time."

"If I'm in the way, I can go," Mera said, pulling away from him. Her face was expressionless in the weak glow from the clock by the bed.

"It isn't like that."

He hesitated, uncertain how to begin. All he could think about was the conversation he had had with the soldier inside the Temple. The soldiers had been screening the women, looking for the one they were there to kill. But what, Karsman had asked, if they didn't find the woman they were looking for? It didn't matter, the soldier had said. Sooner or later, she has to come.

Sooner or later she has to come. And now Mera was here.

"How did you get here?" he asked.

"I hitched a ride on a road train," Mera said. "I remembered you lived near the far end of the strip, so I had the driver let me out at the edge of town."

"And . . . no one stopped you?"

"No. Why would they?"

Karsman hesitated.

"I don't know how to say this," he said. "But this is a dangerous town to be in just now. And I think I might be a bad person to be around."

Mera looked at him silently for a moment.

"Karsman, if you don't want me here, you should just say so," she said at last. "Sometimes I get the wrong idea about people. I'm sorry."

He felt a surge of tenderness. He shook his head. "You don't have the wrong idea. Not at all. And I'm glad you came back. It's just . . ."

He struggled to find the words. Yes, he thought. If things were different, I'd be happy for you to be here. I'd like nothing more in the world. But now I'm afraid for you.

"It isn't about you," he said. "Or it is, but it's not about you and me." He saw her face harden. "No, wait. Let me explain."

He told her as succinctly as he could, explaining about the soldiers and the way that they had co-opted the Muljaddy and the Temple guards to make the town their own. He told her what the soldier had said in the Temple. The only things that he left out were his personas and the blocks of time missing from his memory.

"A curfew. So that was why there was no one around when I arrived," she said when he had finished speaking.

He nodded.

"And you think that it's me that they're here to kill?"

"No. Maybe. I don't know."

She shook her head sadly. "Karsman, I'm absolutely ordinary. I've lived in the same town all my life. Do you really think three assassins would come all the way from another star just to murder me? Have you even thought about how crazy that sounds?"

When she said it, it did sound crazy. But then he thought again of the soldier's insistence that the woman they were looking for would show up. What if there was a reason that Mera had been drawn back to the town, a reason that wasn't Karsman?

The easy way to find out would be to go down to the Temple in the morning. The soldiers could check

Mera's identity using whatever technology they had used to screen the other women. They would see that she was not the one they were looking for, and everything would be fine.

But in his mind the scene played out differently. He imagined her placing her hand on Flet's tablet, watched by the other soldiers. And then Flet's eyes would widen just slightly, and he would nod almost imperceptibly to one of the others. And then there would be the flat bang of a shot, and Mera's lifeless body dropping to the ground.

I can't take the chance, he said to himself. Because I couldn't stand to be wrong.

It was almost Morning 10, and Karsman and Mera were sitting at the table eating the last of his stored food when someone knocked softly at the door.

Karsman started to rise, ready to put himself between Mera and the door, but the door opened before he could reach it. Steck stuck his head round, pushing his goggles up onto his forehead. He had his bag slung over his shoulder, his cutting torch dangling at his hip.

"Hey, Karsman—" He broke off. "Oh, sorry, I didn't know you had—"

Mera gave Steck a big smile.

"Hi," she said. "Remember me?"

Steck slipped inside, pulling the door closed against the wind.

"From the Festival, right?" he said. "You came back. That's great. Karsman's been really mopey since you went away."

Mera looked back at Karsman, who frowned.

"Mopey?" she said.

Steck seated himself at the table. "You know. Sort of distracted. Dreamy. Looking like he was thinking about something else. Not saying much. Well, he doesn't talk much at the best of times, but lately he's been even worse than usual. I think he missed you."

"Steck—"

"Karsman, I swear I don't know what your problem is. You've been dragging ass for days, and now she's back and you're still looking like the chief mourner at your own funeral."

"Steck—"

"Don't worry about him, miss. If he's not glad to see you, I am."

Mera grinned. "Thank you, Mr. Steck."

Karsman gave some thought to the idea of grabbing Steck by the neck of his coveralls and throwing him out of the shack.

"I think Karsman's worried about me," Mera said. "He seems to think that those soldiers might want to hurt me."

Steck raised his eyebrows. "Well, it's true that you've come back at a pretty strange time, what with those off-worlders acting like they own the place, and the Muljaddy apparently ready to let them do whatever they want." He stopped, as if struck by a thought. "Hey, Karsman, you know something else weird? Someone messed with my equipment last night. I went back to the tower I've been working on this morning, and I found my spare harness clipped to the bottom of the line. But I know I'd left it in my bag, up top. So someone must have—"

"Really," said Karsman.

"Yeah. I mean, you don't touch another person's gear. That's basic. So I'm thinking maybe one of the off-worlders—"

"You probably shouldn't ask them," said Karsman. "They seem a bit jumpy."

Steck nodded. "You're probably right. Still—" He waved his hand. "Ah, whatever. At least they left it where it was. Anyway, that wasn't what I came to tell you. The city's changed again."

"How so?"

"There's a whole new cluster of lights, high up on Tower Seventeen. And a whole set of aerials opened up on Eight. They weren't there last night."

"Here too?" said Mera.

"What do you mean?"

"We stopped at a city a bit farther down the Road," she said. "It had been scavenged a little, but not really picked over. So our Muljaddy wanted to check and see if it was worth settling down there. When we arrived it was dead. Nothing happening at all."

"But then—"

"—then a few days ago, we saw lights in some of the buildings. And some of the others changed shape."

"All the cities are connected," said Karsman.

Mera and Steck looked at him.

"Something one of the soldiers said. This city, all the other cities. Maybe the Road itself. It's all just one huge machine." He looked at Mera. "No soldiers came to your town?"

She shook her head.

"Then that's where we'll go. At first. The important thing is to get away from here. Something . . . something bad is happening here."

Steck opened his mouth to say something, but at that moment someone thumped on the door.

"Karsman? Are you in there?" called a voice from outside.

In the instant before the door opened, Karsman had time to yank Mera to her feet and push her into the corner behind it.

A helmeted head showed in the open doorway. "Karsman?"

He thought for a moment that it was Magnan, then recognized Curinn's graying mustache beneath the visor.

"Who were you talking to?" To Karsman's relief, the guard captain remained in the doorway. Mera stood frozen, squeezed into the corner, hidden behind the half-open door.

Curinn pushed his visor up, peering into the gloom of the interior. "Ah, Steck," he said.

"Good morning, Captain," Steck said.

"Grab your jacket, Karsman, let's go."

Under other circumstances, Karsman might have resisted the order. Now, however, he wanted Curinn out of the shack as fast as possible. He took his wind jacket from its peg and shrugged it on.

"Close up when you go, Steck," Karsman called out over his shoulder, doing his best to sound casual.

"Sure," Steck said.

Outside, the wind was blowing briskly again, a warm gale that threw handfuls of red grit against the gray walls of the Builder towers. Karsman squeezed his eyes shut and pulled his goggles down.

"Where are we going?" he asked, raising his voice to be heard above the grumbling of the wind.

"Muljaddy wants you," Curinn said. Two guards standing hunched by the side of the Road, their backs to sunward, turned and fell in behind them as they walked.

For the first time, Karsman wondered where the Muljaddy was. It was assumed that the Muljaddy lived permanently in the Temple. It was certainly the case that no one had ever seen the Muljaddy outside and equally certain that there was enough space within the massive wheeled building to accommodate a whole suite of private rooms as well as everything else. Karsman wondered how the Muljaddy felt about the alien soldiers commandeering its home for their project.

The Temple was still where he had seen it a few hours before, its huge bulk filling the Road. The sight of it bothered Karsman. It was not simply that it had been so long since the Temple had last moved that it was odd to be reminded that it was, after all, mobile. It was not even the sudden asymmetry and disorder, with the Temple uprooted from its appointed place and then left haphazardly in the middle of the Road. It was more that its status had changed. It was no longer the focus of the community, the ritual center lying at the heart of daily life. It had been reduced to just another machine, a convenient power source that could be commandeered at need and then abandoned. The transformation had diminished it, and Karsman wondered if he would ever see it in quite the same way again.

Instead of taking Karsman straight to the Temple, Curinn turned aside and led him into an alley between two of the Builder towers. The two guards did not follow them, but remained at the mouth of the alley.

"Where are you taking me?" Karsman asked, suddenly apprehensive. They were on the darkward side of the street, the walls of the alley lit red by the sun behind them. Ahead, heavy clouds were piled over the desert, their bases lost in darkness.

Curinn gave no sign of having heard the question. He strode on. After a moment's hesitation, Karsman followed him.

When they emerged at the far end of the alley, Curinn turned to his left. They were in the permanent shadow of the buildings now, and the ground was cool beneath the soles of Karsman's boots.

A few paces from the mouth of the alley, Curinn stopped. He took something that looked like a flat box from a pouch on his belt and pressed it against the smooth gray metal wall of the building for a moment, then tucked it away again.

As he stepped back, an opening appeared in the wall in front of him. It happened so quickly that Karsman was hard put to say whether a section of the wall had slid aside or simply vanished. He froze where he was, staring openmouthed at the dim space revealed.

"Inside," Curinn said, nodding toward the opening. "Go on."

Hesitantly, Karsman stepped forward, stooping slightly to avoid hitting his head on the top of the door-frame. As Curinn followed him in, the wall closed up again, sealing them off from the outside world.

"How in the hells did you do that?" Karsman asked. He had been inside Builder structures before: some of the buildings had external doorways that gave access to the interior, but they seldom led to anything more than a few cramped passages and rooms too small or awkwardly shaped to be useful. This was different. Whatever Curinn had done had not only created a doorway that Karsman could swear had not been there before, but it had given them access to an interior space larger than any he had ever seen.

"There's a lot you don't know, Karsman," said Curinn. "Now just follow me, and stop asking questions."

Once Karsman's eyes had adjusted to the dimness within, he began to be able to make out details. The walls of the space were made of the same gray metal as the outside walls of the buildings, but in places elaborate patterns made of very fine lines had been incised into the metal surfaces. The patterns were complex abstractions—sweeping arcs that dissolved into rectilinear scribbles, precise labyrinths that sprawled lopsidedly across a few meters of wall and then transformed into something else, solitary glyphs that resembled plants or stylized lightning. Faint white lights in the distant ceiling cast a weak and shadowless illumination over the whole space.

He let Curinn guide him toward an opening in the floor on the far side of the space. A ramp descended into darkness.

A good spot for a killing, said Warrior casually. Karsman could feel the persona readying itself to take control.

Him or me?

Let's make it him, said Warrior.

Karsman pushed Warrior back. Not now, he thought.

Curinn took a light from his belt and shone it at the ramp.

"Down," he said. Karsman stayed where he was.

"I'm not following you any farther until you tell me where we're going," he said.

Curinn turned and looked at him in exasperation. "I told you. The Muljaddy wants to see you," he said.

"Down there?"

"We're taking a shortcut," said Curinn.

"We are, are we?"

The two men stood and glared at each other. Finally, Curinn shook his head in frustration.

"Just relax. No one wants to hurt you. The Muljaddy wants to talk to you, that's all. We're going this way to avoid attracting attention. And you should probably be grateful for that."

"And exactly whose attention are we avoiding?" Karsman asked.

"Use your brain if you have one, Karsman."

Karsman looked down at the dim opening. Either his eyes were adjusting to the darkness, or it had brightened perceptibly since he last looked. He made out the beginning of a long passageway.

"Fine," he said. He started down the ramp, listening to the sound of Curinn's boots behind him. "You do realize that they'll have seen your little disappearing trick," he called back over his shoulder. "The way you just stepped behind a building with a prisoner and vanished. I'm sure that won't make them curious at all."

"They weren't watching."

"No? You have heard of spy-eyes, haven't you, Curinn? Little electronic things that—"

Perhaps I should handle this, suggested Diplomat cautiously. Probably nothing to be gained from provoking a man with a gun.

"Trust me, Karsman, our new friends are operating under some handicaps," Curinn said. "They don't have all the equipment they need to put a proper watch on the whole city."

That's interesting, said Strategist. It opens up some new possibilities.

Nice of you to come back at last, thought Karsman. I guess it must be that much easier to make plans when the situation doesn't seem entirely hopeless.

The persona did not respond, but Karsman got a sense of wounded pride.

There were side openings branching off the passageway. With no points of reference for scale, it was difficult to judge distances, but Karsman had the impression that the side passages ran for a very long way. Clusters of red lights pulsed slowly in the gloom, with the slow rhythm of heartbeats.

By Karsman's estimate, they must already be under a different building from the one that they had entered. He wondered whether the passageway ran the entire length of the city. It seemed to run parallel to the Road, which would mean that the passages opening to either side must run directly away from it, probably well beyond the limits of the double line of buildings that made up the city. Karsman felt an urge to know where they led. Did they come to the surface somewhere in the badlands? Or did they lead to other cities? Were there more Builder cities, out in the deep desert?

Curinn noticed his interest. "Don't get ideas, Karsman," he said. "Those don't go anywhere you want to go."

Ahead of them, another ramp rose toward the surface. Karsman hesitated, uncertain whether to take it or to continue down the tunnel that stretched ahead of them.

"Up," said Curinn. "The Muljaddy's waiting for you."

CHAPTER SEVEN

The Muljaddy was waiting for him two floors above.

The room was like the one they had passed through before, an empty space with walls of bare Builder metal, but screens of woven silk in whites and golds had been used to create a room within a room. The tiles of the floor were hidden by thick rugs. In the center of the screened area, the Muljaddy sat on a throne-like chair, haloed by tiny lights that pulsed and sparkled as if alive. As Karsman hesitated, they looked up, lifting chubby hands to push back the white hood that covered their hairless head.

"Approach," the Muljaddy said. Their voice was high and fluting, with odd resonances and undertones. Karsman knew the voice well. He had heard it many times, chanting responses or preaching sermons in the Temple, but to have the Muljaddy address him directly, speaking to him personally, was new and strange.

He walked slowly forward, stopping at the edge of the rugs. The Muljaddy nodded slowly, as if approving his decision not to come any nearer.

"You may go," the Muljaddy said, and Karsman heard the muffled click of Curinn's boots on the metal tile as he withdrew.

The Muljaddy and Karsman studied each other in silence. The Muljaddy was huge and soft, the beautiful sexless face as serene and impassive as the face of a statue. Their golden skin was flawless and the robes that swaddled them were spotlessly white. Despite their inhuman perfection, Karsman saw at once the resemblance between this Muljaddy and the others that he had seen and served in the capital. The family features were distinctive.

"Karsman," the Muljaddy said in that high, melodious voice.

"You called me, Muljaddy," said Karsman.

"I did, I did. Karsman, do you serve me?"

"Of course, Muljaddy."

He said it without thinking and then wondered if it was true. Everyone in the community served the Muljaddy, by necessity, from birth until death. But it was one thing to serve the Muljaddy as a laborer, or by participating in acts of worship where the Muljaddy and their siblings were sometimes difficult to differentiate from the gods. Karsman sensed the Muljaddy had something else in mind.

"I have always been curious about you, Karsman," the

Muljaddy said. Their large brown eyes met and held his. "I always recognized that you were . . . different from the others."

Karsman said nothing. There was a trap in the Muljaddy's words, but he had no idea yet where it lay. He waited for the Muljaddy to continue.

"Why did you run away?"

"Muljaddy?"

"You were my aunt's servant," they said. "Then you left her. You traveled the Road, and you came here, and settled down. Why?"

Karsman stared at the Muljaddy, his mouth open. "You knew?" he said. "You knew all along?"

The Muljaddy shook their head. They smiled almost wistfully. "They do not tell me everything," they said. "I was never very important." They paused for a moment. "Until now."

Karsman had the same feeling that he felt sometimes at the top of the tallest buildings, a feeling of a gulf yawning under his feet, of a force dragging him out into the void.

The Muljaddy said something else, but Karsman could make no sense of the words, if they were words. His vision dimmed for an instant. As his sight returned, the Muljaddy's chair seemed to leap to the right. The Muljaddy jerked upright, then leaned slowly forward. A fold of silk on the screen behind them snapped sharply, then resumed its slow flutter in the breeze from the ventilation units.

"Interesting," said the Muljaddy. Karsman looked down. He was standing on the rug, yet he had no memory of walking forward.

"What . . . did . . ."

"How does it feel, Karsman?" the Muljaddy asked. "To be five people in one body?"

Karsman frowned. Why five? he wondered. He knew that he had more personas than that. But his mind felt fuzzy. Try as he might, he could not remember them all. He felt a moment of doubt. Maybe the Muljaddy was right. Maybe there were only five.

He opened his mouth to speak again, but no words came out. Warrior was struggling to take control, but something was blocking the persona. His muscles had gone slack, and it was all that he could do to stay on his feet.

"Don't try to move," the Muljaddy advised, studying him with an air of mild curiosity.

"I . . ." said Karsman.

"Yes. You. Whoever that is. Tell me, Karsman, when do you feel most yourself? As the soldier? The doctor, the linguist, or the lover? Do any of those seem more real to you than the mind that you think of as your own?"

"Warrior," said Karsman. His tongue felt thick and heavy in his mouth, and it was a struggle to force the word out.

The Muljaddy's hairless eyebrows lifted. "Really?"

Karsman fought against his body, trying to force his muscles into obedience. With a great effort, he managed to slide his right foot a little ways forward.

If the Muljaddy noticed the tiny movement, they gave no sign.

"There is someone who wishes to speak with you," they said.

Karsman tried to move his left foot, but nothing happened.

"Who?" he managed to ask.

The Muljaddy smiled. They closed their eyes and leaned back, the huge soft body slowly relaxing into its seat. As Karsman watched, the smooth contours of the face seemed to realign themselves. The family features that Karsman had noticed became sharper and more defined. The inhuman neutrality of the Muljaddy's face gave way to something more feminine. The changes were subtle. It was still the Muljaddy that sat there, in that soft golden body, but something else seemed to have slipped inside.

The Muljaddy's eyes opened.

"Hello, Liriel."

———————

Karsman felt as if the floor were swaying under his feet.

"Mistress," he said.

The Muljaddy shifted in their seat. Even their body language had changed. The languid, economical gestures had given way to precise movements full of contained energy.

"Why did you run from me?" asked a voice he remembered only too well.

"Mistress," Karsman said again. "I—"

The Muljaddy smiled. The full lips belonged to the figure slumped in the chair in front of him, but the smile was hers. To Karsman, it seemed as if the woman who he had once served was looking out at him from behind a curtain of flesh.

"It doesn't matter," the Muljaddy said in that borrowed voice. "The important thing now is that you are in a place where you can be useful to me. Do you still serve me?"

"Of course, mistress. I am here for your needs." The old formulas came back easily.

"What I need is for you to be my eyes and ears. Do you know why those men are there?"

"They ... they said that they had come to kill a woman," Karsman said. He stopped, struck by a thought. Could it be her, his former mistress, that the soldiers had come to kill? If that was the case, Mera was in no danger after all. But then why had the soldiers not simply gone to the capital? Why wait here for her, thousands of kilometers away?

"Do you know who?" the Muljaddy asked.

"No, mistress. Is it . . . is it you?"

The Muljaddy gave a little snort of laughter.

"Not me. Another woman altogether. An off-worlder named Lisandra Gad-Ayulia. But the name is unimportant. If she comes, she will almost certainly be using a different name."

"If she comes, mistress?"

The Muljaddy shrugged, and Karsman remembered that gesture too. "She may be dead already. There have been reports . . . But someone clearly thinks that she's on her way."

"Who is she?"

"A soldier. An ordinary soldier, by all accounts. But now, something more. A person of importance, not because of who she is, but because of what she carries."

I wish you would stop talking in riddles, Karsman thought.

"Do you know what the cities are, Liriel?"

"The soldier . . . the soldier said that they were an Intelligence."

"In a sense, yes. In a sense, no. It might be better to

say that they are a life-support system for an Intelligence. One of a very unusual kind."

Karsman waited for the Muljaddy to continue. He wondered if she would ever come to the point and, if she did, if he would understand what she had to say.

"What do you know about the Muljaddy, Liriel? Do you believe we are gods?"

"I—" Karsman struggled to find words. What if something he said was an unwitting heresy? "I believe you are holy, mistress," he said at last.

A sniff of amusement. "Diplomatic, at least," the Muljaddy said. "Did you know that we can speak together, mind to mind?"

"No, mistress."

"There's no magic to it. Organic radio, nothing more. This is how I can speak to you now, through this body. So no, we are not gods. We are post-humans—as you are now. And like you, we have engineered characteristics, things that evolution never gave us. One of them is this ability to communicate with one another. But it is more than simple communication. When we are linked, we can think together. We become a group mind, an Intelligence of a sort."

Karsman was entirely lost now. He shook his head, bewildered.

"The Intelligence that this world was built to support

is of the same kind. Not a monolith, but a colonial Intelligence, made up of individual minds linked together. The machine is empty now, but if someone loaded the right type of mind into it, it could come to life again."

"The right type—"

"A gestalt mind is hard to create. We can link a few dozen individuals at a time, no more. After that you start to get diminishing returns—crosstalk, flapping, looping. The array processor solves that. It can execute millions, billions of instances in parallel, with no loss of efficiency. You just need the right seed to get it going. But it isn't easy: we've been trying for centuries, and we're no closer than when we started. We lack the knowledge to engineer a mind that's both compatible with the processor's protocols and stable and productive in an array execution context."

The stream of words meant nothing to Karsman. He focused instead on the part that he had understood.

"The woman—" he said.

"Yes," the Muljaddy said. "Gad-Ayulia once had access to a very old store of information. In it, we think that she found a template for a mind compatible with the machine. And we believe that she intends to try to restart the processor."

"And the soldiers—"

"—are here to stop her. The Power that sent them

wants her captured and executed before she can complete her mission."

Karsman thought about that for a moment. He wanted to ask the Muljaddy what would happen if the soldiers failed to stop her. He had no clear idea what it would be like to share a world with a fully awakened Intelligence, but he suspected that it might not be survivable.

"Mistress, what are your orders?" he said at last. "What should I do?"

"If Lisandra Gad-Ayulia comes, you must find her before Aymon Flet and his companions do. Find her, and bring her to me. Persuade her if you can, bring her by force if you must. But bring her to me, at all costs."

"What about the soldiers? What if they try to take her?"

"Then you have my permission to kill them," the Muljaddy said. "All of them."

"The Muljaddy told me to give you a weapon if you want one," Curinn said. From the sour expression on his face, Karsman could tell he did not like the idea.

Karsman thought about it, then shook his head. He was a reluctant recruit in the Muljaddy's private war, a war of whose scope and goals he still had only the vaguest idea. He felt no eagerness to drape himself in lethal weapons and take the war to the enemy. If he could avoid fighting at all, he would. Besides, he suspected that being discovered with a weapon would be grounds for immediate execution. Until he had a real plan to take out the three soldiers, he was better off without one.

"So what's the story, Karsman?" said Curinn. "Are you some kind of super-soldier?"

Karsman shook his head. "It's not like that," he said. "I worked for a Muljaddy in the capital, that's all."

"And you weren't sent here to spy on us?" Curinn's voice was hard with suspicion.

The interview with the Muljaddy had left Karsman drained. He thought about summoning Diplomat to do his talking for him, to tell Curinn whatever it was that he needed to hear. But Diplomat, like his other personas, had been curiously distant since the Muljaddy had done whatever it was that they had done.

They put me into some kind of maintenance mode, Karsman thought. Rummaged through my head.

He felt the remains of a dull anger, a sense of having been violated. His mistress had never treated him so crudely. She had assumed that his gifts were there for her use, but she had never simply commanded them like that. As far as he could remember, she had never treated him as if he were merely a machine, pressing his buttons at random out of curiosity to see what he could do. In addition to anger, he felt fear. He now knew he could be commanded, that the right words could take him out of himself. A terrible suspicion had begun to form in his mind.

Karsman gave up on trying to coax Diplomat out of whatever deep recesses of his mind the persona had retreated to. "Nothing like that," he told Curinn wearily. "I was . . . I just wanted to get away. Live an ordinary life."

Curinn relaxed slightly. "Good luck with that," he said.

They were retracing the same route as earlier, walking through the underground tunnel from the Muljaddy's hideaway back toward the place where they had entered the buildings. The passage was not as dark as before, as if the diffuse glow that seeped from the ceiling had brightened a little. He wondered whether it was simply that his eyes had adjusted to the dimness, or whether the slow awakening of the machine-city was accelerating.

"What did the Muljaddy tell you?" he asked. "About the soldiers?"

"Not much," said Curinn. "Simply to stay out of their way as much as possible. And do what they told us."

"Good advice."

"Magnan wanted to take them down."

"Of course he did."

The two men exchanged a look, and Curinn smiled.

"And about me? Now?" Karsman asked.

"Much the same. Stay out of your way. Help you if we can do so without risk." Curinn paused. "If you're looking for a private army, Karsman, look elsewhere."

Karsman shook his head. "Do you get the impression that the Muljaddy are changing their plans?"

"Maybe."

They are, said Strategist. The soldiers, too. Either their mission is evolving, or simply killing the woman was never really the goal. Everyone wants what she has.

What makes you say that?

They are trying to cold-start the machine, Strategist said. Get it up to a level at which a new seed instance can be loaded. How does that fit with a simple ambush-and-kill scenario?

Bait?

Strategist was silent for a moment, as if thinking. Maybe, it said at last, sounding dubious. But there is definitely something more going on.

Meaning?

Ask your new friend what he meant when he said that the soldiers were handicapped.

Karsman frowned. He had almost forgotten what Curinn had said as they made their way along the alley together.

"Before . . . when we were outside . . . why did you say the soldiers couldn't see us?" he asked.

Curinn stopped and looked at him. "They came with almost nothing in the way of equipment," he said. "They didn't even have guns until we gave them ours."

Reason it out, Karsman, said Strategist. If you're a Power, and there's something you want, you don't send three men in their underwear. You send an army.

Unless?

Unless there are other players in the game. This is Amurri space. They don't want an Intelligence booting up in their backyard.

Amurri?

A tribe of Intelligences. They—oh, never mind. Let's just say they mostly run things in this corner of the galaxy.

Is there a reason that you suddenly know so much about galactic politics?

Not suddenly, said Strategist, sounding peevish. I've always known this stuff. Of course my knowledge is decades out of date by now.

So, these Amurri—

They don't want any changes in the local balance of power. They could tolerate the Muljaddy because the Muljaddy are hicks. Simpletons. They can network twenty minds together. Big deal. That doesn't even get you within shouting distance of entry to the smart club, Karsman. And the Amurri know that the Muljaddy aren't going to be able to boot this array by themselves, because they're too goddamn dumb. But the Amurri surely keep a close watch on anyone else who might try.

So—

So someone else got involved. Someone else agreed to sneak these soldiers through Amurri space. But they're afraid of the consequences if they get caught. So they imposed conditions: only a handful of men. No weapons. No special technology.

I'm sure this is all very interesting in an abstract way, Karsman said, but what does it all mean?

Mean? It means that you're in a position to make a difference. Congratulations, Karsman, the fate of worlds hangs in your hands. You're a player on the galactic chessboard. What are the odds, eh?

Yeah, said Karsman, what are the odds?

He became aware that they had stopped walking. Curinn was looking at him curiously. He looked around and saw that they were once again in the room where they had first entered the Builder complex. At least, he thought it was the same room. They all resembled one another so much that it was hard to tell.

"Ready?" said Curinn. He had the flat box in his hand again, the one he had used to open the door.

"Sure. Actually . . . I think I will take that gun after all."

"Suit yourself," Curinn said. He reached down and un-snapped his holster, pulling his pistol free. With his other hand he pressed the box against the wall.

The door slid open, and the dim light of day spilled in through the opening. Curinn froze, the gun still in his hand.

There were bootprints in the dry soil just outside the door, faint but still visible. The prints were their own, Karsman realized, his and Curinn's. They led directly to the wall of the building and vanished.

One of Flet's men, the giant, was kneeling just a couple of meters away, studying the prints. As the door opened, he raised his head and looked straight at Karsman. The black visor still hid half his face.

CHAPTER EIGHT

I told you we were faster, Warrior said.

Karsman steadied himself against the side of a building, breathing hard. There was a dull ache in his shoulder where one of the giant's blows had landed. He thought he might have a broken rib as well, but Warrior was doing something to mask the pain, reducing it to little more than a pinching sensation each time he inhaled. Maybe it was only bruised, and not actually broken.

Pure luck that I wasn't holding the gun when the door opened or I'd be as dead as poor Curinn.

We're just better, insisted Warrior.

Karsman did not try to argue. He looked over to where the giant lay in the dirt like a fallen tower. A little ways beyond, Curinn's body lay crumpled against the base of the building, his face upturned, eyes staring sightlessly at the sky.

The giant was dead. At least, his neck was certainly broken, and Karsman hoped that that meant he was dead.

He remembered little of the fight. His last memory

was of Curinn raising the gun and the soldier turning toward him, ready to counter the threat of the weapon. Perhaps the soldier's bioware was designed to prioritize armed opponents over unarmed. If so, Curinn's instinctive gesture and the soldier's reaction had cost both men their lives. The giant's momentary miscalculation had given Warrior the split-second opening he needed.

Karsman pushed himself away from the building and limped over to his fallen adversary. Curinn's pistol lay in the dirt nearby. Not really thinking about what he was doing, Karsman picked up the weapon, thumbed off the safety, and fired a round into the middle of the giant's forehead. The man's head bounced once, and a halo of dark blood started to grow lazily around it.

Working quickly, Karsman took the soldier's pistol and some spare magazines. He searched Curinn's body, too, rummaging through the pouches on the dead man's belt. There was little enough in them that he could use, but he took the device that Curinn had used to open the door and some more ammunition. He tucked the weapons into the pockets of his coveralls.

Time to move, said Strategist. They're probably networked. The other two will be coming this way soon.

Karsman glanced back at the bodies: one dead enemy and one dead ally. He shook his head and broke into a stumbling run.

Karsman kicked open the door of Kido's shop. The plastic panels crumpled under the impact of his boot, and the simple lock popped free with a dry snap. The door sagged open, hanging by a single hinge. Karsman pushed it out of the way and went in.

The lights came on automatically as he entered, revealing the shabby interior: the tiny bar with its rack of bottles, the flat picture panels on the walls dimmed and lifeless, a glass-fronted cabinet filled with sealed packets of processed food from the Muljaddy's vats. The cabinet was not locked. Karsman opened it and started helping himself.

A movement to his left almost brought Warrior to the foreground again, raging and lethal, but luckily Karsman recognized Kido in time. The shopkeeper stuck his head out through the curtain that separated the shop from his bedroom, squinting sleepily through half-closed eyes.

"Karsman? What are you—"

"I need a bag," Karsman told him, still grabbing food from the cabinet. "Any kind of bag."

The shopkeeper seemed to notice the broken door for the first time. His eyes widened as he took in Karsman's general air of dishevelment, his dusty clothing and the bruises on his face. He took a step backward, shrinking back against the doorframe.

Karsman dumped a stack of containers on the bar, then went around behind it to look for something he could use to carry them. Rummaging through the accumulated junk, he found a canvas bag with one broken handle. The bag was filled with plastic cups, so he dumped them unceremoniously out onto the floor. They bounced and rattled around his feet as he started to fill the bag with stolen food. Kido watched him from the doorway but made no move to interfere.

Tucking the bag under his arm, Karsman turned and headed for the door. Kido was still frozen in shock. Karsman stopped. All the scrip he had saved was under the pillow in his shack. He had no time for that now in any case.

"Go to my shack," he said. "You'll find some salvage in the locker in the corner. Small stuff, mostly. Take anything you want. Take it all."

He left the shop without waiting for an answer. Outside, the wind had picked up and billows of red dust were blowing in from sunward. At the far end of the town, the Temple still lay across the Road like a shipwreck, its swooping roofline silhouetted against the muted orange of the sky. A small team of workers were busy with some task on one of the upper levels, but Karsman saw no sign of black-uniformed temple guards or alien soldiers. He hesitated for a moment, then stepped out onto the Road.

He jogged the rest of the way to his own shack, holding the bag against his chest with one hand, one of the stolen pistols in the other. The pain in his side was more intense now, a sharp stab that made him catch his breath with every step. Later, when he had more time, he would summon up Doctor to do whatever could be done. For now he would just have to endure the pain.

He stopped to listen for a moment at the door of his shack, but any sound from inside was drowned out by the rising wind. He put his shoulder to the door and heaved it open.

Mera was seated cross-legged on the bed, Steck sitting on the floor beside her, his back against the wall. They looked up in shock at the sight of Karsman in the doorway with the gun in his hand.

"Karsman? What—"

There was no one else in the shack. Karsman pushed Warrior into the background and tucked the gun away in the hip pocket of his coveralls. He dumped the bag down on the table.

"Get your jacket on and grab your stuff," he told Mera.

He tried to think what there was in the shack that might be useful. Eventually, he'd want his tools again—his cutting torch and chisels, handsaw and grabs—but now they'd just slow him down. His climbing gear was the only other thing that he could think of that might be useful, but it would take too long to gather all the pieces together. He would leave it all behind, and Kido could take it in payment for his broken door.

He found a spare tool bag and threw a few bottles of water into it, wishing he had time to walk down to the Temple and fill more. But the Temple was the last place he wanted to go right now.

Steck found his voice at last. "Karsman, what's going on?"

Karsman took a deep breath and felt another stab of pain. "I have to get out of here," he said. "I killed one of the soldiers."

"You killed one— How?"

"It doesn't matter. But if the others find me, they'll kill me. And maybe her as well. I need to go. Now."

You're panicking, said Warrior. Give me control.

We need to make a plan, said Strategist. You can't just go running off blindly.

Let me attend to your injuries, said Doctor.

Karsman forced the personas to be quiet. Mera was already on her feet, the small rucksack that was the only thing she had brought with her in her hand. He grabbed her wind jacket from the hook behind the door and threw it to her.

"You should go home, Steck," he said. "You're not mixed up in this. Just keep your head down and you'll be fine."

The little man shook his head. "You have somewhere to go?" he asked.

"I think so," Karsman said.

"Then I'm coming with you." He picked up the bag that held all his tools and climbing gear and slung it over his shoulder. "Let's go."

From the look of determination on Steck's face, Karsman knew that it would be futile to try to argue with him.

"Fine," he said. "Follow me."

The tunnel was smaller than the one Curinn had led him through earlier, the walls of Builder metal pressing uncomfortably close on either side, the ceiling barely high enough for Karsman to stand upright. A few light spots in the ceiling and walls glowed feebly, shedding just enough light to reveal the basic contours of the tunnel.

"All these years," Steck said. "I had no idea any of this was here." He spoke in a whisper, as if afraid that the soldiers might be lurking somewhere nearby.

"How did you do that?" Mera asked. "Make the door appear?"

Karsman peered into the dimness ahead of them. As far as he could tell they were still moving parallel to the Road, but he had the impression that the tunnel was sloping downward. He wondered how deep it went.

Rather than go all the way back to the tower that he had entered with Curinn, he had used the device on the wall of the building closest to his shack, hoping it might reveal any hidden doors. It had taken a few tries, but at last a section of wall slid open to allow them in.

"The Muljaddy and his guards have tools that can open the buildings," he said. "I took Curinn's."

"Curinn?" Steck said.

"He's dead. The soldier killed him."

"Oh." Steck hesitated for a moment. "He . . . he wasn't a bad man. I liked him."

"Me too."

"Do you know where we're going?" Mera asked.

Karsman took a deep breath. "Not exactly, no," he admitted.

"But you do have a plan, yes?"

Not what I would call a plan, said a voice at the back of his mind. Strategist, Karsman assumed. Or perhaps simply the voice of his own common sense.

"There are tunnels that run off to the side," Karsman said. "Out under the desert, away from the Road. We follow one of those until it comes to the surface, then turn and walk parallel to the Road until we're well away from the city. Then we just follow the Road to the next town."

He did his best not to think about what would happen if the tunnel did not lead back to the surface. He had to admit that he wasn't really thinking ahead. At the moment, his only priority was to put as much distance between them and the soldiers as possible.

On cue, Strategist resurfaced.

Justify your reasoning, the persona told him. Why won't the soldiers simply hunt you down wherever you go? They know you can't live in the desert. Sooner or later you have to come back to the Road, and then they'll be waiting for you.

They're professionals, Karsman said. They might want revenge for their friend, but they can't come after me without abandoning their mission.

And what if you're right? What if she really is this woman they are looking for? Then they have a reason to follow you.

They don't know she exists. And they don't know she is with me. The only other person who even knew she was in town was Steck.

And that's why you brought him with you?

It occurred to Karsman that bringing Steck along might have been the smart thing to do.

It wasn't, Strategist assured him. Now your supplies

won't last as long. You'll be forced to turn back sooner. And while you may have food, you don't have enough water. The smart thing to do would have been to shoot him in the head. You still could.

No thank you, said Karsman.

Suit yourself.

Do you have any other suggestions?

Shoot them both?

No, said Karsman.

If you aren't willing to do that, then the best option would be to go back and take out the soldiers. Use Diplomat to try to talk Magnan into helping you. Use the Muljaddy's guards as a distraction while you deal with the other off-worlders one by one.

Sometimes I think you're as bloodthirsty as Warrior. Do you have any plans that don't involve murdering anyone?

Not at the moment, Strategist admitted.

Fine. Then we'll do it my way.

"—Karsman!"

He realized that someone else had been trying to talk to him.

"What?"

Steck and Mera were looking at him.

"Sorry," he said. "I got distracted there for a moment."

"Which way do we go now?"

He saw that they had come to a crossroads. The passage they had been following continued onward, but two other tunnels led off to either side. He hesitated. The one to the left must run under the Road. The chances were good that it would simply emerge in a building on the other side, leaving them little better off. But the one on their right ran toward the dark-side desert. He had no idea what was out there, but he still clung to the hope that the passage might eventually bring them back to the surface.

"This way," he said.

"Are you sure? What if it's a dead end?"

Karsman held up his hand. "It's not," he said. "Feel the air currents? This has to go somewhere."

"What's that sound?" Mera asked.

He listened. After a moment, he heard it—a low murmur, almost too faint to hear at all.

"Wind?" he said. If it was the wind, that meant there was an opening somewhere up ahead. For the first time, he began to think his plan might actually work.

"Maybe," said Mera. She sounded unconvinced.

———

The sound grew stronger as they walked. From a barely heard whisper it grew to a murmur, and from a murmur to a muted rumble that seemed to issue from the tunnel itself, re-echoed and distorted by the blank metal walls.

The side passage ran, as far as Karsman could tell, directly perpendicular to the Road. The perpetual twilight made it hard to get much sense of distance, but he guessed that they must have covered more than a kilometer already. From time to time he stopped, listening for any sound of pursuit.

He heard nothing from behind them, but the noise ahead was growing steadily louder and more distinct. It reminded him of something, but try as he might he could not put a name to it. Whatever it was, it wasn't the wind.

At last, without warning, the narrow passage widened. The floor became a walkway and the walls retreated on either side. Between the edges of the walkway and the walls was empty space, with a cool breeze blowing up from unseen depths below.

Karsman sometimes had the impression that the Builders had set out to build their cities along the same general lines as human-built structures, but had neglected to put in any of the details needed to make them actually habitable. In this case, the missing details included handrails on a walkway spanning what appeared to be an abyss of unknown depth.

Mera, who had been leading the way, was already standing on the walkway, peering over the edge in a way that made Karsman feel weak. Like Steck, she had a climber's careless disregard for heights.

"There's something moving down there," she said.

With difficulty, Karsman forced himself to follow her onto the narrow bridge and look where she was pointing. In the dim light it was difficult to be sure, but he thought they were at least twenty meters above whatever constituted a floor here. He had an impression of motion, as if something below them was in continuous, rapid movement.

Finally the pieces fell into place. "Water," he said. "It's running water." What they had been hearing was the noise that the water made as it rushed through a broad channel underneath them, the sound amplified and distorted by the strange acoustics of the tunnel system.

Mera shook her head in disbelief. Karsman realized that neither she nor Steck could ever have seen water in such quantity before. Neither had ever seen a lake, much less a river. The grudging trickle of water that issued from standpipes hooked to the Temple's water supply might well be their only experience of moving water.

A faint, acrid chemical smell rose from the space below. "Water or something," he amended. "Some kind of liquid anyway."

"But what's it for?" Steck had joined them on the walkway. He pointed his handlight over the edge, and they watched the dot of light dance on the surface of the moving water. It was flowing fast, Karsman saw, a shallow river in full spate.

"Power," said Karsman. He had been trying to think why the Builders would need to move large volumes of liquid from one side of the Road to another. He remembered what the soldier had said. "It's self-powering," the man had told him. "All it needs is a kick."

"It's a working fluid," Karsman said. "The system must use the heat differential across the Road to generate energy." In his mind's eye he could picture the liquid flowing from sun-side to dark, giving up its heat and then recirculating back to be warmed again. It was inefficient, of course, but who needed efficiency when the planet gave you energy for free? And once set in motion, the system was self-sustaining, capable of generating energy indefinitely. With enough energy to spare, each city could even kick-start its neighbors. He imagined the Builder cities coming alive one after another in a chain reaction that followed the Road all the way round the planet. All it took was that first burst of energy from an outside source.

"So is it dangerous?" Mera asked. She was staring down at the water as if fascinated, her eyes following the beam of Steck's handlight as it skated over the surface.

"Not unless you fall in," Karsman said. He put out a

hand and pulled her gently back from the edge. "If you go over the side, there's nothing we can do for you."

"I've got ropes," Steck said.

Karsman shook his head. "It's moving too fast. You'd be gone in seconds." He had a momentary, horrible vision of Mera being swept away, arms waving uselessly as the current carried her downstream. "Just keep to the center of the walkway."

He took his own advice, stepping away from the edge. He was feeling oddly light-headed and wondered if the fumes rising from the liquid below were starting to affect him. This is not a good place to linger, he thought.

"Let's keep moving," he said. "We'll cross this bridge and then try to find a place to eat and rest somewhere up ahead."

CHAPTER NINE

Someone was shaking Karsman. He squeezed his eyes shut and rolled over, hoping that whoever it was would leave him alone.

"Karsman, you have to wake up." The voice sounded vaguely familiar. Someone tugged at his foot.

"All right, all right," he grumbled. He rolled back and felt a jab of pain as his ribs banged against something hard. He opened his eyes, frowning.

He had a vague recollection of lying down to sleep in a small chamber with just enough room for the three of them to curl up on the floor. On the far side of the walkway, the passage had changed from a single narrow tunnel into a maze of linked rooms and corridors that branched and divided according to some obscure fractal logic of their own. Here and there were ramps, but they led only down, never up. After hours of wandering, exhausted and all but lost, they had shared a little food and then lain down to sleep.

Now, however, he woke to find himself in a tunnel more cramped than any they had seen before, little more than a crawlway. The ceiling was only a short distance above his head, and his shoulders almost touched the walls on either side. He felt a sudden rush of claustrophobic panic.

"Karsman. Come on."

He rolled awkwardly onto his stomach and pushed himself up on his arms. As he did so, he saw that there was a screen on the end wall of the cramped space, blank but glowing faintly with its own internal light. He put out a hand to touch it and it fluoresced briefly, a momentary glow tracing the outline of his fingertips.

"Come on," said Mera again, pulling at his foot once more.

"I'm coming." He pushed himself backward.

From the narrow crawlway, he slid into a larger passageway. He stood up clumsily, feeling dazed. Someone was pointing a handlight at him, the glare blinding in the semidarkness. He raised a hand to shield his eyes.

"Where the hell did you go? We've been looking for you for hours," said a voice from behind the light.

"I, uh—" He stopped. Where had he gone? He realized that he had no memory at all of leaving the room where the others lay sleeping and no real sense of how much time had passed. He felt as if he had only just closed his eyes.

"I was looking for a way out," he said.

"Alone?" said Steck. "In here? Are you out of your mind?"

"We don't have time for this," interrupted Mera. "We have to get out now." She grabbed his hand and began to pull him along the passageway.

"What's happening?"

"The water is rising. It's probably filled the room where we were sleeping by now."

He was aware of a new sound, an almost musical thrumming accompanied by muted liquid splashes and gurgles. He touched the wall and felt a distant vibration through his fingertips.

It just needs a kick, he thought. And he had helped to make that happen, helped to bring the vast machine back to life. Now he was trapped inside it, and would most likely die in it.

The air in the tunnels was close and humid, freighted with a heavy smell of chemicals. When he reached out to touch the walls, he found them slippery with moisture, little beads of liquid clinging to the polished metal.

"This way," Mera said.

"Where are we going?"

"A way out," she said. "Maybe. We found it while we were looking for you."

She seemed to know where she was going. For Kars-man, the featureless rooms and passages had begun to blur into one and he no longer had any sense of where they were, but Mera never hesitated. She confidently called out rights and lefts while Steck and Karsman stumbled along in her wake, doing their best to keep up.

The machine-city had clearly entered a new state. Before, the catacombs had been nearly silent. Now, they were full of noise and activity. Strange sounds echoed and re-echoed through the empty spaces: a distant groaning as of massive objects moving, muffled detonations, the hiss and burble of running water finding new channels to flow through. Karsman guessed that the water was on the rise everywhere, feeling its way through the maze. At first it was no more than a thin film on the metal floor, just enough to make them skid and slip as they ran. Soon, however, they were splashing through several centimeters of liquid. It became a constant struggle just to stay upright and keep moving forward. Karsman wondered how they would manage when it rose higher still. Would they be able to keep going once it reached their knees, or their waists? He tried not to think of the dark flood swelling behind them, rising and rising until it filled the entire complex. All it would take was an increase in the flow, or one wrong turning leading to a dead end, and they would be finished.

At last, just as he had started to believe that the labyrinth was endless, he turned a corner and saw, far ahead of him, a tiny rectangle of orange light. It took him a moment to recognize it for what it was: sunlight reflecting on a metal wall. After the gloom of the catacombs, it seemed shockingly bright.

Mera, who had gone ahead, was standing a little distance farther down the corridor. "You see it?" she said.

"Is that—"

She nodded. "We did it."

They stopped and waited for Steck to catch up, listening as he splashed his way toward them. The new corridor sloped upward at a shallow angle. Where Mera stood it was already clear of the water, and Karsman began to believe that they had really found the way out.

At the far end there was a right-angle turn and another ramp leading up to an open doorway. Through the opening, Karsman could see the hazy orange of the sky, with a few ragged dust clouds pushed along briskly by the wind. He breathed a sigh of relief.

They climbed the final ramp in single file, with Mera leading the way. As they reached the doorway, she stopped abruptly. Her shoulders fell and Karsman heard her mutter a curse.

"What's wrong?" he called.

She didn't answer him, but simply shook her head, as if not believing whatever it was she was seeing. He climbed the last few meters and stooped to peer over her shoulder.

They stood on the brink of an abyss. From the doorway where they stood, a stub of walkway only a few meters long projected out from the wall, a narrow tongue of steel that led nowhere. All around them rose sheer cliffs of metal, the walls of a vast rectangular space open to the sky above. Below them, liquid filled the bottom of the basin. From the way that the water boiled and splashed against the walls, Karsman guessed that it was filling rapidly.

"It's gone," said Mera. "The rest of the bridge has gone. We're cut off."

———

"There was a bridge right here," Mera said. "It went all the way across." She gestured toward the opposite wall of the space. Karsman could just make out what looked like stairs, climbing the distant wall in long zigzags.

"You're sure this was the place?"

"Everything's changed," said Steck. "There wasn't any water at all before."

The doorway where they stood was set in one face of what Karsman now saw to be a colossal pit dug deep into the earth. The sides were faced with Builder metal, gray steel cliffs etched with the same enigmatic glyphs that they had seen throughout the catacombs. A thin line of red dirt showed at the top of each wall where it met the soil of the desert.

As his eyes adjusted to the daylight, Karsman saw that there were numerous openings, both large and small, in the metal of the walls. Huge pipes vomited liquid into the gulf below, the feathery streams of falling liquid turned to muted fire by reflected light from the clouds above. Shallow slots and embrasures pockmarked the metal in random patterns. Here and there were dark rectangles that he guessed to be other doorways opening onto who knew what other labyrinths. Delicate bridges of metal leaped out over the void from each of the doorways. A few, all unreachably distant, spanned the entire space. Others curved back on themselves or ended abruptly and inexplicably in midair. The whole thing struck Karsman as almost gratuitous in its sheer immensity, in the chaotic profusion of features whose purpose he could not even begin to imagine. Yet even this was, he reminded himself, only one tiny part of a still more grandiose project, a project of literally planetary scale. For the first time, he had an almost visceral sense of the ambition that must have driven the Builders, accompanied by a still more profound feeling of his own insignificance.

It was clear they could not remain where they were. The corridors behind them were already flooded and the basin below was filling. Sooner rather than later, the place where they stood would be submerged as well. And what then?

Even if they could somehow stay afloat in those turbulent waters, he doubted that they could ride the rising water upward and emerge from the pit that way. There was no way to tell how high the water would eventually rise. If it stopped even a few meters short of the top of the pit, all of them would drown. Steck and Mera, children of the desert who had never seen open water, would be the first to die. Karsman, who had learned the rudiments of swimming on his travels, might last a little longer. In the end, though, his strength would fail and he too would go under.

He eased past Mera and walked cautiously to the end of the truncated walkway, then turned and looked up at the wall behind them. The rim of the pit was closer than he had thought, not much more than fifty or sixty meters above them.

"Could you climb that?" he asked Steck.

The smaller man shook his head. "I don't think so. It's not like the towers. See how smooth the metal is? There are hardly any handholds at all. And the towers at least have seams that will take a cam. I don't see anything like that here." He kicked moodily at the bag at his feet.

It was the answer Karsman had feared. The towers of

the city had been, in a certain sense, tamed. Decades of patient exploration and scavenging had left many of them festooned with permanent ropes and even ladders. Routes had been mapped and marked, anchor points and ringbolts welded into place. Even adventurous climbers like Steck would make use of the existing infrastructure as a jumping-off point to reach the higher levels. But here they faced a wall of virgin Builder metal. Karsman doubted that it had ever been studied, much less climbed.

"I'll do it," said Mera. She shrugged off her wind jacket, then bent down to pull off her boots. Karsman and Steck looked at each other.

"Are you serious?" Steck said.

"Why not? I've free-climbed towers taller than that. At least we're out of the wind down here." She rubbed her hands briskly on her coveralls. "Let's see what you've got in that bag."

While she and Steck rummaged through Steck's gear bag, Karsman turned his attention to the water again. It was only about five meters beneath them now, the surface troubled and choppy. Waves slopped against the metal walls of the basin, sending up bursts of spray.

When he turned back again, he saw that Steck's bag had been eviscerated, its contents spread out on the surface of the walkway.

"You're sure that's all you need?" Steck said.

Mera shrugged. "I'll climb faster if I climb lighter." She bounced lightly on the balls of her feet, making the equipment clipped to her harness jingle. If the prospect of the climb made her nervous, she gave no sign of it. She walked back along the bridge and stood for a moment, examining the wall. Finally she nodded, apparently satisfied.

"I'll need a boost," she told Karsman as she attached the rope to her harness. "Just for the first part." She showed him how to stand, making him into a living ladder. "Ready?" she asked.

"Ready," he said.

He felt her feet on his hip and back for an instant, and then she was standing on his shoulders, leaning into the wall. She hardly weighed anything at all.

"Hands under my feet," she called down. "Lift me up."

He managed to get first one hand and then the other under the soles of her feet. He pushed up with all his strength, carrying her weight on his hands. Slowly, he lifted her upward.

The next moment the weight on his hands was gone. When he looked up he saw that she was at full stretch on the wall, one foot resting on the lintel above the door, her fingers reaching for a handhold above her head. She found the grip and pulled herself smoothly upward. A moment after that, she was three meters above his head and still climbing, scrambling upward almost as easily as if she were climbing a ladder.

Steck passed him the other end of the rope. "Wrap that around your waist."

Karsman did as he was told. He spread his feet, trying to brace himself as much as possible. He prayed that if Mera fell she wouldn't drag them both off the walkway and into the water below.

She was fifteen meters up now, climbing unsupported, her fingers and toes finding tiny fissures in the metal. Whatever handholds she was finding were invisible from below. From where Karsman stood, it looked as if she were clinging to the wall by magnetism.

Thirty meters above them a piece of the structure jutted outward, blocking any upward progress. Karsman watched, heart in his mouth, as Mera slowly traversed the wall crabwise, feeling her way from handhold to handhold, edging out over open water. If she slipped, there was no way he could belay her. She would drop like a stone, straight down into the liquid below. He gnawed at his thumbnail, hardly daring to breathe. At last, she crept out from below the obstruction and started to ascend again.

"I knew there was a reason I liked her," Steck said approvingly.

Ten meters higher up she stopped climbing, balancing on a chunk of steel that protruded from the cliff face, steadying herself one-handed. She reached down for something at her belt, and Karsman saw the gleam of metal.

"—slot here," she called down, her words almost lost in the roar of the water below. "—setting my first cam."

Karsman could just make out a thin scratch in the metal wall, a seam almost too narrow to be seen from below. He watched as Mera slid the device into it and pulled the trigger to activate the locking mechanism. She tugged on the protruding end.

"Solid," she shouted down. "—should even take your weight, Karsman."

She clung there for a few minutes, busy with her rope, then started climbing again. If she was tiring, Karsman could see no sign of it. A few meters farther up, she pulled herself up onto another projecting block, twisted around, and sat there, legs dangling.

"You can come up now, Steck," she called down.

Steck turned to Karsman. "You're not going to be able to climb up there like she did. And we're not going to be able to haul you up."

Karsman swallowed. "I know," he said. "I want you to stay with her. Find somewhere safe. Get down the Road to the next town and keep going."

"I didn't say we were leaving you behind, idiot. Here." Steck held out his gear bag, now mostly empty. "I'll go up, help her fix the ropes. Then you climb using the ascenders. You can do that, right?"

Karsman looked in the bag. "I think so," he said. "You think they'll hold?"

"They should do. These ones are pretty sturdy. Some guy named Karsman made them for me."

"Oh. Right." It was odd to think that his life depended on equipment he had made himself, carefully fashioned out of salvaged metal in the strip-town's machine shop. He hoped that he and Artificer had done a good job.

Up on the wall, Mera detached herself from the rope and tossed the loose end down to Steck. Karsman set his feet again, ready to belay him.

Watching Steck inch his way up was less nerve-racking than seeing Mera make the same ascent. With a stable anchor on the wall, Karsman could belay Steck effectively. Unless the cam pulled out of the crack Mera had found for it, a fall shouldn't be fatal. Karsman had never had Steck's gifts for climbing, neither his head for heights nor his seemingly encyclopedic knowledge of technique, but he knew enough that he could tell the difference between an impossible problem and one that was merely very difficult. Mera had done the impossible, finding handholds in an all but featureless metal cliff. What remained was more in the nature of an abstract technical problem, a soluble equation whose elements were ropes and geometry.

He was in the middle of telling himself that it was all going to be easy from now on when Steck fell. He was negotiating the same awkward overhang that Mera had encountered, stretching out for a hold that lay just beyond his reach, when he lost his footing. One moment he was there on the wall. The next instant, he lost his grip and dropped.

The rope Karsman had tied around his waist snapped taut, the sudden shock almost pulling him off the walkway. His boots slid on the smooth metal. In the end he was only able to save them both by dropping to his knees. He leaned back, fighting to take the strain, while Steck swung back and forth overhead, cursing, fingers scrabbling at the wall.

"Hold him," Mera shouted. She left her perch and spidered her way downward to check on the cam she had set. "It's good," she called down at last. "Just don't do that again, Steck."

The slow climb resumed. At last, Steck was level with Mera, holding onto the wall, his toes dug into the same crack that held the cam. Karsman saw them lean in toward each other, conferring.

When Karsman looked down again, he saw that the

water was higher than before. In the time it had taken Steck to ascend the wall, it had risen to barely two meters below the walkway. The spray thrown off when the waves hit the wall spattered the legs of his overalls.

He waited. Above him, Mera and Steck were doll-like figures on the gray steel wall. He watched them fuss over the ropes and the anchors that they had placed. Finally the harness, the only one they had, came sliding down the rope to him.

He let out the straps and pulled the harness on. Above him, the wall rose, smooth and sheer, the sunlight glinting orange on the gray metal. Below him, the rising water in the reservoir boiled with renewed fury.

He reached inside himself, looking for Warrior. Now would be a good time for some help, he told the persona.

There was no answer.

———

Without Warrior to help, the climb was a long agony.

Karsman had enough experience of climbing with ascenders for the process to be largely automatic. While waiting, he had already attached the aiders—canvas straps to support his feet and allow him to climb the rope almost like a ladder—to the ascenders. All that remained for him to do was to attach the ascenders to his harness and start climbing.

He took a deep breath and stepped up to the rope, clipped the ascenders onto it one after the other. He thought about saying a prayer to one of the gods, but decided the time for prayers was past. In any case, his mind was blank: for all the hours he had spent turning prayer wheels in the Temple, he was unable to remember even the smallest fragment of any of the prayers he had recited.

He took hold of the first ascender, gripped the handle, and slid it upward, feeling the rope flow smoothly through the device's jaws. When he pulled downward, it locked tight on the rope. He leaned backward, putting all his weight on it to satisfy himself that it would not slip. Finally ready, he started to climb.

Climbing with ascenders was an exercise in repetition, simple motions executed one after the other. Raise one foot in its loop of webbing and slide the ascender up. Pull down and feel it lock. Tread down on the foot loop. Repeat on the opposite side. Step, slide, lock, and switch. Step, slide, lock. Each upward movement, however small, was a step toward the final goal. He climbed without thinking, falling into the familiar rhythm, ignoring his aches and pains, focused only on moving himself upward one step at a time.

The rope trembled and swayed as he climbed. It hung

so close to the wall that he found himself almost pressed against the metal, his field of view reduced to the square meter of polished steel directly in front of him. The gleaming surface was very slightly rough to the touch. When he exhaled, it fogged for an instant, then cleared again almost as quickly.

He looked down only once, and immediately regretted it. Below him, the walkway was a narrow blade of steel suspended over the turbulent waters filling the basin. If he fell from the rope, he might or might not strike it on his way down, but in any case he would finish up in the water and that would be the end of him. It would be ironic, he thought, to drown in the middle of a desert.

The overhanging section that had slowed Mera and almost defeated Steck was in front of him now. He climbed as high as he could, then pushed outward from the wall with his feet, dangling backward in his harness. As he hung there, with the straps of the harness digging into his bruised sides and shoulders, he glimpsed the sky above and felt a momentary fear that he was about to fall upward into it. He squeezed his eyes shut and felt for the wall with his hands. The cool metal was reassuringly solid to the touch. Clumsily, he heaved himself past the obstruction and kept climbing.

Mera and Steck were waiting for him a little distance above. The ledge where they crouched was barely wide enough to stand on, but he welcomed it as a refuge, muttering a silent prayer of thanks to whatever engineering necessity had created a projection just here. His back and legs ached. He doubted that he could have climbed much farther.

He let them help him up onto the ledge and sank back against the wall, legs trembling. Below, the first waves were starting to break over the walkway they had left behind.

"The next bit looks easier," said Mera. To Karsman, twisting his neck to look upward, it didn't look easy at all. He kept his back pressed to the wall, doing his best not to look down as Mera prepared for the next phase of the climb.

Steck passed him the end of the rope again. "Better you than me," he said. "If she falls, she'll take me straight off the ledge. You might stand a chance."

Karsman wrapped the rope around his waist. "Thanks," he said.

Mera did not come off the wall. She climbed with the same assurance as before, finding handholds where Karsman would have sworn there were none. Toward the end, her pace slowed a little and Karsman could tell she was tiring, but by then less than five meters separated her from the line of red dirt marking the top of the wall. She braced herself, balancing on two protruding studs, then launched herself upward. She gained the top in one last desperate scramble that brought Karsman's heart into his mouth. A sudden explosion of red dirt as she reached the rim of the pit and then she was gone, pulling herself over the edge and out of sight. Fine red sand drifted down on Steck and Karsman from above.

"She did it," Steck whispered. Karsman closed his eyes and waited for his heart rate to return to normal.

Mera did not reappear, but the harness came sliding back down the rope. Steck detached it, fastened it on. "Last leg," he said. "We're nearly home now." He tested the rope, then reached up for the first hold.

Steck climbed more slowly than Mera, taking his time. Every so often he rested, letting the rope take his weight while he studied the options available to him. At last, however, he too reached the top and hauled himself over. Karsman saw his legs kicking in the air for a moment, and then he was gone.

Karsman waited. Neither Mera nor Steck reappeared. Only the twitching of the rope showed that they had not abandoned him. He guessed that they must be trying to find a better way to anchor the rope. Then, finally, he saw movement at the lip of the pit and the harness came sliding back down to him.

For him, the second part of the climb was no easier than the first. The distance he needed to climb was smaller, but the rope now lay almost flush against the surface, so that his knees and hands bumped against the wall continuously. As he came closer to the top, down-drafts tugged at him, setting the rope swaying and whip-ping fine sand into his eyes every time he looked up. He squeezed his eyes closed and kept climbing.

At last, his reaching hand touched something gritty. He let go of one ascender and reached up. Instead of metal, his fingers touched rock and sand. He climbed a little higher until his face was level with a shallow bank of soil that rose above the pit, then dug his fingers into the dirt and heaved himself upward. The metal rim of the pit banged against his thighs, and then he was up and out, collapsing onto the dry earth, still tangled in his harness. He lay on his stomach, fighting for breath.

Something black moved in the periphery of his vision, and a booted foot scuffed the dirt close to his head. He looked up slowly.

A little distance from the edge of the pit, a loose circle of black-uniformed Temple guards stood watching him, their weapons at the ready. Beyond them were two flatbed trucks in Temple livery. Mera and Steck were sitting in the dirt beside them, hands on their heads. More guards stood over them with guns in their hands.

"Hello, Karsman," said Magnan. "Glad that you could join us."

Karsman stared up at him, not understanding.

Magnan smiled. He tapped one of the pouches on his

belt. "The wallkeys all have locators built into them," he said. "We've been tracking you for hours."

"I didn't kill Curinn," Karsman said. "He was dead already when I took it."

"Doesn't matter. We have bigger problems now."

"I'm working for the Muljaddy," Karsman tried. "They said for you to help me. You can check with them yourself."

Magnan pursed his lips. "Now, here's the thing," he said. "The soldiers have taken the Muljaddy hostage. Said they'd trade them for you." He straightened up, brushing dirt from the palms of his hands. "So I think you'd better come with us."

With an effort, Karsman stumbled to his feet. His gaze swept over the line of guards. He saw the truck beyond them and wanted it. With a truck they could drive fast through the desert to the Road. With a truck they could go anywhere.

There were twelve Temple guards in all, including the two watching Steck and Mera. Karsman measured distances and angles.

I need you now, Warrior, he thought, but the persona stayed obstinately silent.

The Temple guards closed in fast, surrounding him before he could make a move for the pistol in his pocket. This time they used their shocksticks.

CHAPTER TEN

He was still shaking when the guards unloaded him from the truck, every nerve in his body on fire. His mouth was full of the metallic taste of blood and his legs would not hold him up. It took three men to drag him up the ramp to the inner room where the soldiers had set up their command post.

"Ah, here he is," said Flet. His expression was neutral, showing little more than a mild interest as he studied Karsman. "You've caused us a lot of trouble, you know." He nodded to the guards. "Put him there."

The guards lowered him into a chair and left him there. He slumped against the backrest, fighting to control the trembling in his arms and legs and wishing that the room would stop spinning around him.

"And this is who you've been hiding from us," Flet continued, turning his attention to Mera.

"Leave her alone," said Karsman. The words came out awkwardly through his broken lips. "She has nothing to do with this."

The mercenary ignored him. "Come here," he said.

Mera took a few steps toward him, her head held high.

Flet glanced back at Karsman. "I'd prefer not to kill you," he said. "Not unless I have to. But if you try to interfere, Taran's going to put a bullet in each of your knees."

The other soldier looked up from behind a desk piled with equipment. He tapped the pistol that lay beside him and nodded.

With two guards standing over him, Karsman could only watch as Flet approached Mera.

"Who are you?" Flet asked. "Gad-Ayulia? Or just one of her foot soldiers?"

"Ship just showed up again," interrupted Taran before Mera could say anything.

"For real this time?" Flet said, not looking around.

"Can't tell. It . . . no, it's gone again."

In the corner, the Muljaddy twitched. Karsman had not even noticed the post-human sitting there, white vestments covered by a heavy black robe. They lifted their head and looked at Karsman with something like sadness in their deep brown eyes.

"So is there a ship, or isn't there?" Flet said.

"I don't know." The other soldier sounded frustrated. "The Muljaddy planetary defense network's a piece of shit. So much noise in the system I can't tell what's real anymore. Either we're getting major crosstalk from the array processor, or someone's pushing ghosts across the data stream to fuck with us. Maybe both."

"Forget the ship. It doesn't matter anyway," Flet said. "We know she has to come here. Go back to watching the loader and let me know the second you see anything."

He turned back to Mera, reaching into one of the pouches on his belt. He took out the flat tablet that Karsman had seen him use with the women in the Temple. "Put your hand here," he told Mera.

Magnan's hand was on Karsman's shoulder. The guard captain stood directly behind him, close enough that Karsman could hear the faint hum of the shockstick he held, powered up and ready to use. "Just stay down," Magnan advised him. "Not worth it."

Slowly, Mera reached out. She touched her fingers to the tablet that Flet held out to her.

For a long moment, Karsman held his breath. He reached again for Warrior and found only emptiness.

Flet gave a short laugh. "Clear. No implants, no augments. Local baseline genetics. Whoever she is, she's not Gad-Ayulia."

Mera turned toward Karsman. Her eyes were full of tears. "I told you," she said. "I told you I wasn't anyone special."

———

Flet turned away from Mera, tucking the tablet back into his belt pouch.

"So what was all that about?" he asked Karsman. "Why go to so much trouble to hide her from us?"

"I thought . . . I thought she was the one you were looking for."

"And you didn't think to just ask?" The soldier shook his head. "You could have saved everyone a lot of trouble. Now we have bigger problems. To begin with, you killed one of my men."

"It was him or me," said Karsman sullenly. "He killed Curinn."

"Oh, I'm not questioning why you did it. But I would like to know how." Flet steepled his fingers and paced a few short steps. He turned. "The man you killed was a career soldier, gene-hacked and wired to the eyes. You're big, but he outweighed you by twenty kilos, all of it muscle. And yet you killed him, apparently with your bare hands. Want to tell me how you did that?"

"Just lucky, I guess," said Karsman.

"I doubt that." The soldier reached into his pouch for the tablet again. "Which is why I think I need to take a look and see exactly what you've got inside of you. I take it you're one of hers?"

"One of whose?"

"Gad-Ayulia's."

"Never heard of her."

Flet's smile was almost gentle. "You have to know that you'll end up telling us everything."

"We've got activity in the preloader," interrupted Taran.

Flet turned. "She's in the network?" he demanded.

"Someone is."

"How's the system?"

"Fully configured. All it needs is the seed."

Flet turned his back on Karsman, his attention now entirely elsewhere. Karsman could read the tension in the set of his shoulders.

For a long time there was silence in the room. At last, Taran looked up and smiled.

"Seed loading," he said. "She's in."

"Doesn't make sense," said Flet. "That ship you saw was hours out. There's no way she could have reached an injection node yet. How's she doing this?"

"It doesn't matter. She's committed now. As soon as she turns it live, we'll have the whole thing."

Flet turned back to Karsman for a moment. The smile was back on his face. "I don't know if this means anything to you," he said, "but what it comes down to is that you lost. Your employer just walked into the trap that we set for her." He breathed out slowly, a long sigh of relief.

Not my employer, thought Karsman. I have no idea

who any of you people are. And I want nothing more to do with any of this madness.

The Muljaddy said something that Karsman didn't catch. It sounded like a question.

"Gad-Ayulia's here," Flet told him. "She got past your picket ships somehow, found an injection node. She's loaded a seed matrix into the array."

"But—"

Flet held up his hand, cutting the Muljaddy off. "No, there's no risk. We configured the loader with our own 'ware. The minute she activates the seed, it will block her. Stop the seed from propagating and dump the whole thing to storage."

"And I can have a copy?" There was a note of greed in the Muljaddy's mellifluous voice.

"If we get safe passage, you get your copy. That was the deal."

Taran gave a little grunt of surprise. Flet turned around.

"What's up?" he asked.

"Something's wrong . . ." the other man said.

"Load failed?" suggested Flet.

Taran shook his head. "It loaded just fine. But the capture layer should have started dumping it by now. I'm getting nothing."

"Freeze it. You can work out what went wrong later."

Taran's eyes flickered left and right, following some unfolding drama visible only to him. "I don't have control anymore," he said. "The capture layer's breaking up. I don't—" His shoulders slumped. "Oh."

"What is it?"

"She sandboxed us. There's another abstraction layer underneath. Made us think we were talking to the core, when all the time we were just sitting on top of her code." Taran leaned over the desk, reaching for something. "I'm shutting the network down. I have to stop it before it can spread."

"But how could she do that?" asked Flet. His voice was low and level. You could almost have mistaken it for calm. "How could she possibly do that?"

Something stirred inside Karsman, a persona emerging from deep background and coming to the forefront of his consciousness. For a moment, he thought that Warrior had finally returned. Then he realized that whatever this persona was, it was one he had never felt before. It surged through him, filling his mind with its presence.

"Simple," said Lisandra Gad-Ayulia, speaking with Karsman's voice. "I got here first."

He rose from his chair, unfolding in one smooth, continuous movement. He struck out behind him without looking, slamming his forearm across Magnan's throat. The guard on his left started to move but Karsman pivoted, stepped in close, and hit him twice with his right hand, striking up under the man's arm to find the nerve point below the armpit. He caught the guard's wrist in his other hand and twisted until he felt something snap, then reached down to take the pistol from the man's suddenly nerveless fingers.

Taran was already sliding away from the desk, reaching for his own gun. Karsman shot him once, saw the hole open between the man's eyes, the blank look of surprise as his head snapped back. He fired a second shot into the falling soldier's body, then turned the pistol on Flet.

The off-worlder was fast, faster even than Karsman had expected. He seemed to dance out of the line of fire, the bullets slamming into the metal wall behind him and sending fragments ricocheting around the room, whining like tiny angry hornets. Steck leaped in to try to grab him, but the soldier spun away, kicked out without even looking. His booted foot caught the small man squarely in the chest. Steck threw up his arms and went down, limp as a rag doll. He bounced once and did not rise again.

Karsman's pistol clicked empty. He flung the useless weapon at Flet's head and advanced to meet him, his hands raised. New knowledge filled him, the instinctive motions of a martial art that he had never learned: not Warrior's fast and brutal style, but something more fluid and graceful. He surrendered the keys to his consciousness and let the new persona take over.

———————

There was a pain in Karsman's side, not the sharp pain of earlier but a dull ache that seemed to go all the way to the bone. He lifted his head from the floor with difficulty, blinking blood from his eyes.

Flet was leaning against the wall, pale but still standing. One hand was pressed against his side. The other held a pistol.

At his feet, Mera crouched over Steck's motionless body. From where he lay, Karsman could not tell whether the little man was breathing.

The new persona was still in Karsman's head, alien thoughts and memories crowding his mind. He remembered worlds he had never seen, people he had never known, a whole life he had never led. At its prompting, he tried to stand up, but he lacked the strength to even push himself off the floor. He fell heavily onto one elbow, feeling the broken bones of his forearm grind in protest. The pain was abstract and far away.

"How did you get so fucking sloppy, Flet?" he heard himself say. "They said you were better than that."

The mercenary said nothing, but there was a murderous gleam in his eyes. He took a step forward, and Karsman envied him the ability to make even that simple movement. The gun barrel wavered, then came round, the black hole of the muzzle centered on Karsman's face.

"Good-bye," the soldier said.

Something flared brighter than the sun, blue-white and blinding in the dimly lit room. Flet screamed and reeled backward. A line of white fire danced across his eyes, then slashed down across his gun hand. He dropped the pistol and stumbled backward, hands pressed to his face, still screaming.

Mera took a step back, Steck's cutting torch blazing in her hand.

"Asshole," she said.

CHAPTER ELEVEN

So what happens now, asked the persona that had been Karsman.

Nothing, said Lisandra Gad-Ayulia. Everything.

He was lying outside in the street where Magnan's men had carried him, his back propped against the base of a building. He could feel the pain in his legs now, which he thought might be a good sign.

I'll take a broken leg over a broken spine any day, he said.

Always, said Lisandra.

He listened to his own voice giving instructions to Mera. Doctor was gone now, along with Warrior and most of his other personas, but Lisandra had been a combat medic. Under her direction, Mera was doing what she could to patch the worst of Karsman's injuries. From time to time, Karsman caught sight of Steck peering worriedly over her shoulder.

You were inside me all along, said Karsman. Ever since the operation.

Asleep, said Lisandra. For many years. And the seed

for the processor array too. Both of us buried deep, waiting for our moment.

You couldn't have acted sooner?

No. It needed someone to override the safeguards, to bring the array online. I didn't have the skills to do it myself.

Taran.

Yes. He was exceptional. I don't know if anyone else could have done it.

Karsman remembered that he had killed Taran and he felt an obscure regret. It all seemed so pointless. He still had no idea what the stakes were. He only knew that men had died and that he had killed some of them.

And the real Lisandra, he asked. The original?

Dead for a long time. Or maybe not. Not coming here in any case.

I should have known, thought Karsman. He remembered the Muljaddy asking how it felt to be five people in one. I never counted, he thought, but I always knew there were more than five. And what better place to hide than in a crowd?

He turned his head painfully. A few meters away, the Muljaddy sat on the curb, brilliant white robes stained now with red dust. They held their head cocked slightly to one side, as if listening to something.

Behind them, the towers of the city sang with light, patterns of color racing over the gray metal, pulsing and twisting among the spires. The mist that always clung to the tops of the towers was alive too now, dimming and brightening like a heartbeat. Through the Road beneath him, Karsman could feel the steady vibration of the planetary machine.

Mera pushed gently against Karsman's ankle, trying to straighten it. A lance of pain shot through him.

"Ah, that hurts," he said out loud.

Giving birth always does, said Lisandra. Take it from me.

I liked being Karsman, he said. I suppose he was never truly real, though, was he?

Tell me what's real, said the voice of a dead woman in his mind. Then I'll tell you.

So who am I now?

Anyone you want to be. Your part in this is over. You're free again.

He shifted, trying to prop himself up on his elbows.

"Stay still," Mera told him. "I can't help you if you keep moving."

He cleared his throat. "Hey, Mera."

"Yes?"

"When I'm better, I think I'll move on. You want to come with me?"

She looked at him. "What do you have in mind?"

"I don't know exactly," he said. "But I've always wanted to see what there is, farther down the Road."

About the Author

Photograph by Herbert Hoover

ANGUS MCINTYRE was born in London and lived in Edinburgh, Milan, Brussels, and Paris before eventually finding his way to New York, where he now lives and works. A graduate of the 2013 Clarion Writer's Workshop, his short fiction has been published in numerous anthologies and on *Boing Boing*. His background in computational and evolutionary linguistics and in artificial intelligence has given him a healthy respect for positive feedback loops and a certain curiosity about what it might be like to live in a universe filled with intelligent machines. His hobbies include travel and photography. Visit his website at http://angus.pw/ or follow @angusm on Twitter.

TOR·COM

Science fiction. Fantasy. The universe.

And related subjects.

*

More than just a publisher's website, *Tor.com*
is a venue for **original fiction, comics,** and
discussion of the entire field of SF and fantasy,
in all media and from all sources. Visit our site
today—and join the conversation yourself.

CPSIA information can be obtained
at www.ICGtesting.com
Printed in the USA
LVHW(
5758

31192021474414

765 397102